Dominique

Her Tale of Love

ALEXANDRA OYELOLA

Contents

DEDICATED

To every girl or boy, far away from the
safety of home…

Intro

Cowering at the side, the girl watched as the men approached her, and she shivered at the thought of what they would do to her. She knew what they had come for and their capabilities, but she remained wary.

A slap cut across her cheek, snapping her out of her resistance. Looking up, she glared at the men. Tears had long ceased to be her reaction to this assault. She had no idea if she knew how to cry anymore. Some time ago, she recalled, she would weep and beg for their mercy, but this did not change them. Thus, she found no usefulness in pleading.

"Open those legs of yours!"

She glared at the man who had made this statement, her eyes dancing over his lanky stature. He was coarse and filthy. Men were filth and a mistake of the creation. Why did God accede to forming men in the first instance? These creatures were not humans but savage animals. Men, being the ones with power, strength, and authority, did nothing more but spread the oblivion rule of being the greater ones.

Females were nothing but the lesser ones, the unwanted ones, and the common ones. Indisputably, they were second in everything. This indifference was born when the first humans were created. Millions of years have gone by, but the curse of being female still burned fiercely through the world.

Just like every other vulnerable girl child out there, she was also a part of the curse. Her name was Dominique, and she had no surname. She was an orphan raised by a woman she had always known as Dinah, popularly known as *Mama Di*, the owner of the prominent motel she currently served in.

Most in and around the brothel referred to Dominique as 'Mini,' referencing her smallish stature instead of the typical 'Minnie.' Although, standing at 5'2 didn't mean she was a dwarf. Her birth date was unknown, but Dinah hinted that she was brought into the world seventeen years ago.

Her job in the brothel began four years ago. Yes, she was just a young adolescent then, and it was a crime to join the world of prostitution at that age. But she had to concede to this, as she had no other option. She was young, naive, and alone. What could she have done to protect herself and survive the harsh world?

Minnie's first experience was the day she was presumed to have clocked the age of thirteen, and the one who despoiled her was none other than John, Mama Di's only son.

* * *

Four years earlier, Minnie lay on the floor, which served as the pleasure of bed space. A slight touch came over her naked lap. Startled, she jumped up only to meet with the dark eyes of eighteen-year-old John.

"Bro. John?" she questioned.

The young man ignored her and began unzipping his brown shorts.

Slapped to reality, she rubbed her eyes, but she was in no dream. Taking her by surprise, he enveloped her tiny body in his arms under his hot breath.

"You are so sexy and pure." He breathed as he cocked his head to her neck, trailing hot kisses down her collarbone, his scaly lips blistering her soft skin.

Working his hands to her back, he undressed her from the pink gown she had on.

Minnie tried to fight his hands off, but they were strong, and her little fights just turned into wriggling in his grip.

Suddenly, his hips found a way with hers, and she gasped. Her body went numb at the alien feeling that rushed through her. She struggled to repress her muffles as she felt something hard pierce her. Unable to hold the agony, she screamed, but John was quick to clasp his palm over her mouth.

He continued rocking his hips with hers, and all she could do was weep silently. Her body was stupefied, and all she could feel was the coagulating sensation between her legs. Each second, her thighs seemed to stretch and open. All she perceived at that moment was the movement of his body against hers and the angst feeling in her stomach.

After an eternity of moans and muffles from her and John, she felt the cold release within herself and the pronounced sigh that followed from John.

Instantly, he rolled off her. She was breathless, dazed, and trapped in the spot. Her little mind could not comprehend his actions as she stared into the nothingness ahead.

John rose to his feet, gathered his clothes, and walked out of the room, abandoning the shaken Minnie. When the magnitude of what had happened hit her, the waterfalls in her eyes broke as she wept. Despite her age, and her ignorance of the adult world, Minnie was well aware that this was wrong, very wrong. Alas, there she was, seconds after her first sexual experience with the boy she had long called her brother.

But, despite how hard she cried, she could not rid herself of the burning pain in her chest, nor could she express how dirty she felt. At that moment, she was despoiled, vulnerable, and different. She hated John, she hated men, and she sincerely hated herself.

After crying her eyes out, she pulled herself to her wobbly feet and dragged her body to the washroom. She tried for several minutes to wash off the feeling, but no scouring could wash away the truth.

Glancing between her legs, she noticed red stains stuck to the inner sides of her thighs, but she simply washed them off, too dazed to care.

The door to the bathroom creaked open, and through her glassy eyes, Minnie saw Mama Di stride in.

"How long do you plan on washing and weeping?" she asked with a voice stern as always, only softening at the mention of money.

Trembling, Minnie blurted out, "Ma, John forced me." She couldn't keep this to herself. She was scared and confused. She was in dire need of the comfort of a mother's hug.

Mama Di crossed her arms in front of her huge chest as she frowned. "And, what?"

The words slapped Minnie hard, and her heart fell to her stomach. Blinking repeatedly, Minnie tried to convince herself that she was hallucinating, but reality whacked her in the face when Mama Di spoke again.

"You should be glad that he was gentle with you, considering your age," Mama Di hissed.

Minnie felt her heart thud on hearing Dinah's words.

"When you're through scrubbing, meet me at the balcony," the woman added before stepping out of the washroom.

Minnie's jaw fell, and her eyes remained frozen as she stared at the door. She could not ignore the obvious: Mama Di had something to do with John's actions. What's more, she might be the author of his actions.

She knew Dinah had never loved her, but Minnie did. She loved Dinah all her life. Even though the feeling was unrequited, Minnie believed she cared for her. After all, Dinah was the only motherly figure she had in her life. But Dinah had never loved her, nor did she give a damn about her. Minnie was just another street kid, abandoned and neglected by those who ushered her into the world.

Since Minnie was a little girl, she had longed to know her biological parents, but now, she wished she had never met them. She was alone in this world and had accepted that. She was cursed by those she thought she could love – this was imprinted as a scar in her mind. Now, she had been robbed of what little dignity she had left. What more had she got to lose?

Burying herself in the bathtub, she hoped the cool water would fill her lungs and end her struggle, but she gagged instantly. At that moment, even death didn't seem to favor her.

This was the actuality of whom she had turned into and the beginning of her miseries.

The following day, Minnie began her journey as a child whore, or whatever could describe a thirteen-year-old girl having intercourse with men for cash.

As a full-fledged whore, she had to look good at all times. She had to act well and be obedient to all those rotten dogs and pigs that patronized the brothel, each paying for a moment to drill someone who might be the age of their child. The best was that she had to smile – every morning – at the man she hated the most, the one who took her virtue. And, for years to come, she knew she would continuously have to bathe in this facade for as long as she remained a commercial sex slave.

* * *

Back to the present, her latest reality, the men took their turns having their pleasure off her body, ensuring that they satisfied their urges and cladding up before leaving the room.

Minnie also stood to her feet and pulled her nightgown back on. This wasn't a new thing to her. This was the daily routine of her life. All she ever did was be with men, and because she had no trouble getting lustful glances thrown at her, she was always engaged with one client or the other.

Other girls in the brothel sometimes complained of having lesser clients or having to please fragile old men. Parenthetically, she had done this too. One main fact about her was she was the only one in the brothel who had to be with seven men on the go. Despite being a young adult, and the youngest in the brothel, she seemed to be the queen of whoring, and the one doing the impossible. This was her ill-starred jinx.

She walked out of the room and into the open yard. Tonight was a busy night as every girl seemed to have someone with her.

Finally, she got to the entrance of her room and stepped in. She immediately ripped her clothes off before diving into the bathroom and burying herself in the cool refreshing water.

"Minnie!" Dinah's voice cut through her tranquility, and she cursed under her breath.

The madam was there to commend her on her additional action of sex tourism.

Stepping out of the tub, she grabbed a towel from the rack and draped it around her body. Although, it was pointless trying to cover what had been seen by many as she had walked around naked. However, for the sake of sanity, she had to array herself.

On returning to the room, Minnie sighted Mama Di on the bed, counting wads of notes in her hand with so much interest her lips were tugged into a full smile.

"Minnie, those men paid handsomely. You did a good job, they said," Dinah praised. It was sickening to watch Dinah compliment her on her iniquitous exertion. However, despite her loath, Minnie pulled on a tight-lipped smile.

"That's good to hear, Mama," Minnie replied.

After ensuring that the notes were properly counted, Dinah stretched out some to Minnie, who collected them with her plastered-on smile.

"Thanks, Mama."

Dinah shook her head. "You are welcome, my little Mini," she commented and exited the room.

As soon as she left, Minnie's smile fell, replaced by a feeling of repugnance.

"Thank you for ruining my life, Mama," she muttered.

Minnie moved to the cabinet under her dressing mirror and pulled out a miniature, dark-blue box. She shoved the naira notes she had just received from Dinah into the container, which held other various monies.

Resolutely, Minnie looked into the space ahead as her jaw became firm, and her grip on the box tightened. She had to get out of the brothel as soon as she could. Life was out there, she knew. There was a lot more to the world, which she craved to see, and this would be her only chance at freedom. She had anticipated this day for as long as she could remember, and finally, the day had come. Now, she could get her ass out of the brothel, as staying even a second longer was more than torture.

As much as she knew that the world reeked of wickedness and hatred, she was certain that there were other amazing feelings outside the walls, and she had to experience them.

Flinging her wardrobe open, Minnie began throwing her outfits onto the bed. She had to travel light, so she aimed to take only what she needed. She stuffed everything into a black box before cramming the contents and closing it up.

Minnie immediately changed into something more decent and walked out of the room with the box. Carefully, she made her way to the side of the huge walls to a slight opening caused by an accident involving one of the drunken clients. The man reportedly had a cracked skull and some other broken bones, but all thanks to his stupidity, she now had a chance at escaping.

Squeezing through the hole, she pulled her box along and made it out. As she looked up, she was hit by a fresh breath of freedom. This was it! At last, she was departing from Dinah's prison. Her destination might be unknown, but it was better to be lost in whatever was out there than to stay another second on these premises.

Taking one last look at the brothel, she spat on the ground and spun around before strolling down the street, dragging her box along with her.

One

That night, Minnie left her small town on a bus, and in the wee hours of the following morning, they got to Lagos, the city that never sleeps.

Upon alighting, Minnie looked around as the other passengers began finding their way home while she stood beside the bus, unsure of her next move or destination.

Lagos had been discussed widely among the girls back at the brothel, and it was portrayed as the "golden city" where dreams came true. Truly, Lagos was a beautiful city. Its streets were filled with diversity where vehicles cruised along, disturbing the air with their horns and curses as they began their daily activity. Everyone was doing something or going somewhere, all except Minnie, as she stood and watched.

Clinging to her box, Minnie glanced around. To her right were taxis and commercial motorbikes. Their respective drivers and riders called out to her, offering to convey her to her destination, wherever that might be. To her left were several shops.

"Where are you heading to?" A charming voice brought her out of her thoughts.

She spun only to be met by a well-built man clad in a white vest over blue jeans and a black leather jacket. His outfit hugged his body perfectly, highlighting his abs and his manliness. Yet, despite his sexy appearance and gorgeous smile, Minnie was far from interested in conversing with him.

To remain polite, she forced a laugh. "Nowhere," she wheezed.

In a softer tone, he added, "But you can't stay here. You ought to have a place to go."

Despite his kindness, she became irritated. "I'll find my way, thank you," she said through gritted teeth, trying her best not to sound impolite or pissed

He pressed on. "You can't stay here, miss. It is quite dangerous," he stated.

Minnie rolled her eyes and scoffed. "I said I will find my way!"

Her voice blared through the atmosphere, and everyone threw their eyes at them.

The biker looked around and returned his eyes to her. He muttered an apology before he withdrew himself to his group. She swallowed hard on realizing she was too harsh on him, but he just refused to understand that she wasn't in the mood to accept his offer of assistance.

Her tummy rumbled, causing her to ignore him as she turned around, searching for a food vendor. Luckily, a kiosk was a few meters from the cluster of bikers.

After buying from the kiosk, she sat on the side tabs, munching on the sausage roll she had bought, along with a bottle of chilled Coke. Anyone looking at her would probably mistake her for a ravished dog as she devoured the rolls instantly.

Several passersby glanced at her. She could not tell if they were surprised at her way of eating or her mode of dressing.

Taking the latter into consideration, she observed her outfit: a simple purple crop top imprinted with the words 'Fuck off, assholes' donned over black ripped jeans. Yes, she had to admit that the words on her top were vulgar, but how she chose to dress shouldn't be anyone's concern. So, she threw them a scowl, and they looked away.

After sitting at the same spot for three hours, she decided to walk on, hoping to find her way to somewhere, anywhere, just as long as it wasn't where she currently was.

Strutting down the road, she noticed a small street by the side, and she turned in that direction dragging her box with her. Some boys sat on the side of the road, and from a glance, Minnie could ascertain they were thugs from their outfits and the smugness on their faces.

As she walked on, she noticed how they looked at her. She tensed up and quickened her pace.

The boys stood up and followed. She gulped as her breathing increased rapidly. Looking back, she saw they were still on her trail. Trying to get farther from them, she turned her pace into a jog. But she tripped on her left foot and fell to the ground.

They got to her, encircling her in their midst.

"Well, aren't you a fast one?" one of the boys stated, and the others erupted into laughs.

"Idiots!" she cussed, her gaze directed downwards as she inspected her ankle, suspecting she was hurt.

She felt heat rise to her cheeks, and the cords in her neck became rigid and firm. Throwing her eyes back up, she glared at the boys. "What do you want?"

Ignoring her, another boy reached for her box, but Minnie prevented him by hitting his face with her palm.

"We've got a fierce one!" the boy announced to his friends, and they all closed in on her.

She tried moving away from them. She couldn't allow them to cart away her possessions. Neither would she let them get any other thoughts.

"Stay away from me, or else…" she yelled.

The boy who had initially spoken up crossed his arms, and a smirk appeared. He questioned, "Or else what?"

Minnie's glance darted from the boys to her box, her heart pounding hard against her ribs. What was she to do? She couldn't face them all. They were nine strong boys and only her. Still, she wasn't planning on losing to those amateur thieves, and she'd fight them with all she had.

Roars of bikes interrupted her thoughts, and she shot her eyes at the source of the coordinated noise. It seemed she wasn't the only one taken aback by the sounds of the bikers as the boys also turned to look. But, on seeing the men on the bikes, the boys immediately scampered away, abandoning her and her things.

Minnie looked up to the heavens in prayer, thankful for narrowly escaping a mob.

One of the bikers, the one who led the team, alighted from his bike and walked up to her. On removing his helmet, Minnie felt a sharp twang in her chest as she recognized the rider. She couldn't miss that sharp jawline, honey-brown eyes, and that sexy mesomorph body embedded with abs like those of the gods. It was the biker she had earlier yelled at. On a full scan, Minnie couldn't deny how gorgeous he looked.

"Are you okay?" he inquired; his forehead puckered.

Minnie nodded.

The corners of his lips turned up, and he added, "You sure you're not hurt?"

Minnie hummed, satisfaction swelling in her chest. "I am not hurt, thank you."

He extended his hand to her, offering to help her up, but she stared at his hand, biting the inside of her cheek as she considered taking his help. She instantly thought against this and shook her head slightly, declining his help. She placed her palms on the ground and pushed herself up, but the piercing pain from her ankle shrilled down her spine, and she felt a line of sweat between her brows. This, however, caused her to stumble backward, but a pair of strong arms caught her in time.

His voice came as a whisper to her ear, and his breath was warm on her skin. "Your ankle is injured. You need to have it checked."

Minnie couldn't afford to go to a hospital. She did not have enough funds for that. So, she turned down his offer with a polite 'No.'

He pursed his lips, his brows furrowed into a frown on noticing her hesitation. "I know you don't want my help—"

Minnie chimed in before he could complete his sentence. "Correction," she started as she separated herself from his grip, placing her body on her perfectly good foot. "I don't need your help. I can very much handle myself," she boasted.

Without sparing him another look, she picked up her fallen box and tried to stomp away from him, but she stumbled on her hurt leg. However, this time, he didn't save her from falling, and her butt met with the hard ground, and she winced.

The other bikers crooned into rhythmical laughter at her fall. As she gazed at the face of the biker, she noticed the upward quirk of his lips, and she realized that he was smothering his laughter. She frowned and looked away from them, knowing she couldn't hide the blush that crept onto her face.

His voice came up behind her. "Can I help you now?"

She rolled her eyes. There was no way she could get back to the main road without his help. So, reluctantly, she bit her lower lip as she agreed. "Fine."

His mouth twitched into a smile, and he marveled at her acceptance. "Great." Bending over to her, he placed his hand around her back and gently hoisted her onto his bike before he also got on. The others followed suit on their respective motorcycles and rode on – leaving Minnie and her mysterious knight.

"Hold on tight," he advised, gesturing to his waist.

Minnie stiffened at the thought of wrapping her arms around him, and begrudgingly, she did as she was told. On looking at the front mirror of the bike, she caught the smug look he had as he rode on, speeding onto the main road.

* * *

After several moments of hair blowing, wind gushing, and a heart-thumping ride, the bikes drove into the premises of a private clinic. Looking up at the sign, Minnie cringed on noticing the name 'St. John.' Her lower lips quivered as John's image flashed in her mind. Despite the mere coincidence, Minnie couldn't help but let her emotions overwhelm her as she stiffened up.

The biker parked his motorbike under the only shed on the premises, which served as the hospital's garage spot. He got down and helped her off his bike.

Minnie followed the biker's gaze at the multi-level hospital.

He cocked his head to her, and in a little voice, he asked, "May I?"

She nodded. After all, her ego was already squashed a little, and more wouldn't kill her.

He immediately whipped her into his arms effortlessly. "You're quite light for your appearance," he said.

She scowled at him. "Was that supposed to be a compliment, or did you just insult me?"

The corner of his mouth quirked up as he laughed. "Neither. It is just a harmless observation."

As soon as they got in, the unwaged nurses stood and rushed to them, two dragging with them a stretcher. Terror overtook Minnie on seeing the stretcher. This was something she had partnered with people who had died, so she couldn't let them lay her down on it.

"I'm not laying on that thing!" she snapped at the nurses. "I'm not dead."

Their faces scrunched up, and they tried to dispute her statement.

Minnie frowned. She was about to retort, but the biker cut her to that.

"It's okay. We'll need the doctor a.s.a.p.," he mentioned, saving the nurses from her tongue-lashing.

The nurses led the way into a large consulting room, and the rider gently placed Minnie on the bed. This surpassed what she had thought, but he had been acting better than she had expected. He was nice, so unlike the others.

"Sir, you'll have to leave," one of the nurses pointed out, and the biker stepped out of the room, and the rest followed suit, leaving Minnie alone in the white-walled room.

Almost immediately, a man in a white coat walked in and straight to the side of the bed. He inspected her ankle, which had begun to swell, the skin around the affected area turning red.

"Does it still ache you?" he inquired as he touched the sides of the bloating ankle, and Minnie winced.

"It does," she answered.

He nodded and jotted something onto the writing pad in his hand before inviting one of the nurses into the room.

On coming in, he whispered something to her while they both looked at his pad.

The nurse stepped out, and not too long after. She returned with a tray filled with drugs. Minnie wrinkled her nose, and she stuck out her tongue, her hatred for drugs curling into her system. No matter how cute a color they came, drugs remained her worst enemy.

"Must I take them?" she coaxed.

The doctor lifted an eyebrow, puzzled at her question, but still, he nodded.

"They are for the easing of your pains. You'll need them for a speedy recovery," he explained.

Minnie pouted. "Fine!"

The doctor prescribed the necessary dosage, and she took them unwillingly.

Shortly after, she felt the heaviness in her eyelids. Fighting the tiredness, she tried to keep her eyes open. She wondered what the drugs contained, as it felt like she was drugged. Unable to keep her eyes open, she closed them and fell into a deep sleep.

* * *

Chatters of birds snapped Minnie out of her sleep as she tore her eyes open. Instantly, she was met with milky walls, and her body tensed up — she wasn't in the consultation room anymore.

Looking around, she noticed she was in a room. Her leg was elevated, and a small compression bandage wrapped around her ankle. Digging deeper, she saw that her stuff was missing, and so was the bike dude. Panicking, she gaped. Could he have been a thief? If so, it would explain why he was so nice to her.

Tears filled her eyes, and her nose burned at the thought of getting robbed. How was she to pay the hospital bills and survive the city with no penny in her hands?

The only door to the room screeched open, startling Minnie out of her thoughts. She threw her eyes to the doorway. A slim nurse walked in. Minnie relaxed as she saw that it wasn't some intruder. But how could anyone be an intruder in a hospital? As rare as that could be, Minnie preferred to believe it was a possibility.

Noticing that Minnie was awake, the nurse smiled. "You're awake, miss?"

Not reciprocating the smile, Minnie asked, "Where is the dude that had brought me in?"

The Nurse's forehead creased, and she shook her head. "I just resumed my shift, and I haven't seen anyone here," she admitted.

Minnie's brows drew together at the Nurse's words. "Just resumed? But how is that possible? I was just brought in here a few minutes ago."

The Nurse's eyes crinkled at the edges as she grinned. "Not at all, miss. I am a morning-shift nurse, and I resumed seeing you already admitted."

Her eyes went wide. "Do you mean I've used a whole day here sleeping?"

The nurse chuckled. "You have been admitted for a total of twenty-two hours."

Minnie blinked and gaped. "I can't believe this. How did I sleep for that long?" she retorted.

The nurse's grin dissolved into a warm smile, and she continued, "You were prescribed a very effective pain reliever, and this made you sleep for that long." This she explained as she pulled out a syringe from the bedside-crate and infused the contents into the I.V bag connected to Minnie's arm. At that moment, Minnie realized that a drip was linked to her.

"You need to eat something, miss," the nurse added.

Minnie nodded, although she had no idea how she could get something edible to eat when she had just been robbed of everything she had. She squeezed her eyes shut as she tried to think of her next action. She was seventeen, alone in a huge city with nobody she could call hers.

"Well, you are here," the nurse said to someone.

This made Minnie flutter, her eyes open as she focused on the doorway.

The rider walked in, her lips parted open, letting out a huge exhalation of her pent-up breath on seeing him. He was there, and he hadn't run away.

His lips tugged into a smile as he walked toward her. "You're up. How is your ankle?"

"Uh, I'm okay," she hurriedly replied, her eyes surveying him to see if he had her belongings.

He probably noticed as his smile deepened.

"Hey, your box is safe," he assured.

Minnie's insides brightened up at this. At least she still had her things.

Adding in, he asked, "Did you think I'll let them get stolen?"

She lowered her gaze in embarrassment, remembering she had called him a thief.

Plastering a smile on her face, she looked up and said, "Can I see them now?"

Surprised, his eyebrows rose, but he quickly covered this up with a thin laugh. "They are at my place," he replied.

"Your place?" she echoed, disappointed that he didn't have her things with him.

He joked, "Yes, my place. I didn't just fall from the skies, did I?"

Minnie shrugged off his joke as she remained serious.

Noticing this, he straightened up and added, "You'll be discharged in the afternoon."

This revelation caused her heart to skip a beat. How could she settle her bills? This had been on her mind ever since she woke to see herself admitted.

"Alright." She sighed. "How much was charged?" She gulped, preparing herself for the blow of the exorbitant charges, but the rider only smiled in amusement.

He cocked his head to hers, and in a soft voice, he breezed, "That's not an issue. I've settled them."

Minnie's jaw fell as his last sentence rang in her ears. Did he pay her bills?

* * *

To her knowledge, motor bikers weren't full of cash, and thus she wondered how he could have afforded to pay her bills. More importantly, why did he do this much for someone he barely knew?

"You settled the bills? Why would you do that?" she questioned, just to confirm the dude had gone completely bonkers.

He shrugged, and she kept her eyes on him while wondering why he would do that for her.

"Okay, I'll pay you back!" she stated.

The corners of his lips twitched into a wide smile. "Well, of course, you will."

The air around her dampened as his words echoed in her ears, and her face burned hot. She just knew it. He was too good to be true. There was no such thing as goodness. He was just like the rest, looking for a way to get in with her.

"Forget it!" She scowled at him, and his smile slipped. "You can as well go ask for a refund!"

His eyes were frozen open as he stared at her — completely shocked at her outburst. He blinked, and his lips parted as he gasped. "Geez. Fire." He raised his arms. "You've got a hot temperance."

Minnie laughed in disbelief. "Hot temperance?" Her laugh dried up immediately, and she glared, pulling herself up from the bed. "I'll show you hot temperance." She sneered at him, and he backed away.

"Okay," he stuttered. "You are so feisty."

Minnie exhaled as she calmed herself, knowing that any further actions and she'd have herself to blame. But anger still burned within as she glared at him.

The biker pressed his lips together. "If you're so upset about repaying, then you'll just have to cool off," he said.

Minnie shot her eyes at him and saw that he was leaning on the adjacent wall.

"I was only joking," he pointed out.

Under her breath, she scoffed. "Asshole!"

This was so low that the biker couldn't have heard her. Maybe she had misjudged his words, but could she be blamed? After all, this was what men expected from girls like her.

"What will you eat?" he asked.

Minnie looked up, unblinking at what he had just asked after she had just taken her anger out on him.

"Uh, speaking to me?"

He laughed. "There are only two of us in this room."

She pursed her lips, ensuring it was well pronounced. "I thought you were speaking to the walls or to your ego that just got squashed." She sniffed.

He laughed again. "My ego's doing pretty fine, but my stomach isn't. It's been growling like a mad lion for a while now, and I'm sure you haven't eaten a thing, too, right?"

Minnie stared at him, her eyes half-closed.

Seeing that she didn't reply to him, he said, "Just save it. I'll get you something," And he turned to leave.

Minnie called him. "Wait! I don't even know you."

He glanced at her with a smile on his lips. "Formalities shall be attended to later."

"What's your name?" she asked.

"Alexander," he answered and threw a wink at her before vanishing out the door.

Minnie stared at the door, wondering who he was and why he was helping her. God knew how much she had disliked him and how badly she had judged him, but despite it all, he remained helpful. Even if his thoughts were pure,

Minnie couldn't bring herself to trust him. However, she was thankful that he had saved her.

* * *

A while later, the door opened, and Alexander walked in, and in his hands were two takeaway packs.

"Phew, I can't wait to stock my mouth with everything in here," he muttered as he placed her a pack.

She mumbled a slight "Thank you."

"No, thank you." He smiled. "I was dying to go into that cafeteria, but they wouldn't serve until one claimed to be buying food for a patient."

Minnie couldn't help herself, and she laughed.

The corners of his eyes crinkled as his lips stretched into a broad smile. "You look good in laughs," he complimented.

Minnie looked at his face and noticed that his eyes were on her. Immediately, her laugh died, and she replaced it with a scowl.

He sighed. "But I guess that's gone now."

Ignoring him, she dug into her meal: fried rice garnished with fried plantains and sliced beef. She knew she was starved, and this was obvious from the way she rushed the food.

After she had eaten, the doctor came in and injected another serum into the IV beside her.

Sleep had always been her favorite hobby, and no matter what, sleep never let her down. It just felt like the doctor was purposely drugging her to sleep with whatever he kept injecting into her drip.

Still, despite her hard-headedness, not even a few minutes later, she was soon fast asleep. She was a slave to her slumber.

* * *

The shuffling of someone's legs caused her to jump out of her sleep as she heard silent whispers.

"Are we sure this is her?"

"Quiet down."

"Yeah, shish."

The voices sounded so close to her, and her body hair stood in fear. She fluttered her eyes open and caught sight of the four men in the room with her. She almost flew out of her skin on seeing the alien men, but she did not fail to yell, "Who the hell are you?!"

Four pairs of eyes sprang to her at once, and from a guess, Minnie could tell they were surprised by her reaction. Yet, one of them approached her, and she moved back.

"We're—"

Minnie didn't give him a chance to explain. She threw him another question. "What are you cheese brains doing in my room?"

She expected a reply from the men, but Alexander's voice came into her ears instead.

"They are here to pack up," he stated as he appeared from behind them. "We're discharged," he added.

"We are?" Minnie questioned.

He answered, "Yes, we are."

Minnie's heart skipped a beat. *Discharged? This means I could leave the hospital, but where am I supposed to go—?*

Cutting into her thoughts, one of the men, a hunky giant with a hideous tattoo of a scorpion on his right arm, said to Alexander, "Alex, we ought to go now."

Alexander replied, "We'll be leaving in a while, Oak."

Making a mental note to question the hunk's name later, Minnie frowned. Where were they heading to, and was she accompanying them? It was not as if she wanted to be anywhere near them, but she couldn't help but let the thoughts of 'what next' bother her.

"Are you set?" Alexander asked her.

Caught unawares, she stuttered, "Uh?"

He smiled. "We have to go."

Unable to hold herself, Minnie asked, "Where?"

The men all laughed, but all it took to shut them up was a scowl from her, and they instantly quieted.

"Fire, we're heading home," Alexander replied.

Minnie raised an eyebrow. "Home?"

Alexander pursed his lips. "Yes, home. My home," he said before his forehead scrunched up, and he asked, "Or, do you have someone we can drop you off at?"

She bit her lower lip and reluctantly said, "You can drop me off where you had picked me up."

Alexander laughed. "Yeah, that's not happening."

Minnie frowned. "What do you mean?"

Facing her, he explained, "I am not going to let you go back there and wait additional millions of days." His eyes gazed at her. "We've got space, and you could hang around till you get yours," he added, and a small smile curved up his lips. "Is this alright with you, Fire?"

Minnie stared at him, completely lost for words. She had been nothing but hostile to him, but he was inviting her to squat in with him and his dudes. Yes, she needed his help, but she didn't trust him or anyone else enough to follow them to their house. After all, they will probably take advantage of her once she looks helpless.

Even if she did consider his offer, she knew he must want something in return.

"And, what would you probably want in return for a while in your home, Alexander?" she inquired.

He walked towards her and brought his face close to hers, and in a small whisper, he said, "Nothing."

Minnie snapped her eyes to him at once. How could he want nothing in return?

"Nothing?" she questioned.

"Yes, nothing. I've learned that you loathe the words 'payback,'" he replied.

She rolled her eyes and, in a low voice, muttered, "Okay."

Standing straight, he smiled, satisfied with himself. "Now that 'her majesty' has decided, we can be on our way."

Alexander offered to help her up, and she knew better than to reject his help. She could barely feel her foot, and if she attempted to stand on her own, she would definitely fall.

On agreeing, he hoisted her into his arms, and they all walked out of the hospital.

Minnie looked around for their bikes, but there weren't any on the premises. All she could see were several cars, and a jeep parked just a few meters from the building. She eyed the vehicles, wondering if they belonged to Alexander and his friends, but this wasn't possible. They were riders, after all.

Yet, her jaw flung to the ground when the hunk opened the jeep's passenger door, and Alexander placed her carefully on the seat. The others filed into the back while Alexander moved over to the driver's seat.

Unable to hold her curiosity, she asked, "Alexander, where are your bikes?"

The men at the back laughed, and the hunk spoke up, "I'm guessing that you've missed the wheels."

Minnie threw him a scowl, and he instantly looked away.

Chuckling, Alexander replied, "It's alright, Fire. We're going home in this baby." Dropping his voice to a small whisper, he added, "Alex is fine. You don't need to sound so formal with me."

Minnie rolled her eyes at him, scoffing under her breath. The sound of the engine roaring to life brought her face to him, and she met his eyes.

He asked, "Ready?"

She ignored him and looked out the window, but not before she caught the slight smirk on his lips. Taking one last look at the hospital, she sighed as the jeep drove out of the premises.

Two

Throughout the entire ride, Minnie kept to herself as she stared out the window, watching the road speed past them. However, the guys were engrossed in their conversations and jokes, but she tuned them out. She had no idea who they were, from Alexander to his friends. But there she was, accompanying them to God knew where. She did not trust them, but she didn't have another option. Either she left with them, or she slept on the streets. The latter was nearly impossible, as the government had banned the loitering of homeless individuals.

The jeep drove off the main road, taking a corner down the street. From the outlook of the housing, setting, and people around, Minnie could tell they had just driven into a typical Lagos slum. She couldn't say that she hadn't expected Alexander and his friends to come from the ghettoes, but after seeing the jeep, she had begun to think otherwise. But, in the end, she was right. They were shantytown kids.

The drive came to a stop in front of a four-story building. As soon as the car stopped, children from around came gushing at the jeep, yelling at the top of their voices. Minnie winced at their loudness. She never liked children and only wondered how anyone could cope with those tiny monsters. Nonetheless, she was glad she wasn't going to have any. How could she when she wasn't planning on having anything to do with blokes?

"Fire?" Alexander called her out of her thoughts, and she turned her eyes to him. "Are you coming down, or do you need more time to smell the car?"

Minnie scoffed at this, and he laughed.

Looking to the back, she saw that the four were already out of the jeep. Alexander also alighted, walked over to her side, and helped her out. On stepping down, Minnie was met with little rascals' faces surrounding them. They stared at her as if she was some alien from another planet.

But she couldn't care less what the children thought of her.

"Guys," Alexander faced the children. "We've got a visitor, and we wouldn't want to disturb her now, would we?"

The children all shook their heads.

He smiled. "So, we'll chat later."

Surprisingly, they all turned and ran off, their trumpeted screams echoing down the road. Minnie let out a breath of relief. She'd never understand kids.

Turning to her, Alexander said, "Shall we?"

She pursed her lips and replied, "Whatever."

He scooped her into his arms, and they all walked into the building.

* * *

On entering, Minnie noticed several people loitering around and judging from the way the guys exchanged pleasantries with them. They were very well acquainted with one another. This only increased her unease as she realized she was the odd one out.

They all stared at her as Alexander carried her up the stairs until they got to the top floor.

A slightly-older lady walked out of the house, and her eyes immediately landed on the girl in Alexander's arms. Her forehead wrinkled as she kept her gaze fixated on the alien presence in their midst. "Who is she?"

The hunk replied from behind them, "Mom, she's Alex's friend."

Minnie blinked. So, this was Oak's mother, and most likely, Alexander's too, if they were brothers. However, this was only her assumption. She couldn't be sure and wasn't about to ask.

The lady's lips stretched out into a warm smile as she walked toward them.

"So, what shall we call you, Alex's friend?"

Taken aback by her question, Minnie blurted, "Uh?"

"She meant your name, missy," the hunk pointed out, and she shot him a glare, but he laughed.

Ignoring him, Minnie smiled at the woman and answered, "I'm Dominique, but you can call me Minnie."

Alexander turned to her, and under his breath, he repeated after her, "Dominique."

At that moment, she realized that she hadn't even introduced herself to him, even after knowing his name. This made her even more perplexed that he went ahead to help a girl he did not know.

"That's a beautiful name, Dominique," the lady commented. "I'm Esther, Noah's mother," she introduced herself.

Minnie finally figured that Oak was a nickname for Noah.

"Alexander is a big part of our family, and so all his friends are always welcome." Esther said, her smile deepening, and she added, "You are welcome, Dominique."

"Thanks," Minnie said, wondering what Esther meant by Alexander being a big part of their family.

Alexander cleared his throat, making everyone turn their attention to him, including the girl in his arms. "Esther, can we continue this later? I'm not exactly a superman," he stated, and everyone laughed.

"Of course, Alex. We still need you and your arms." Esther chuckled. "We'll see you both at dinner."

"Yes, ma'am," Alexander replied.

Minnie threw the lady a smile as he took her further into the house, only stopping at the entrance to a room.

"You've got a beautiful name, Dominique," he remarked as he pushed the door open.

Minnie rolled her eyes at him, totally giving him the cold shoulder.

Glancing around her, she gasped at the neatness and beautiful arrangement of the room. It was well-painted and had a pleasant flowery smell to it. She doubted that this was his room. This could never be his room, which was a relief to her, as she could not imagine sharing a room with him or any of his cocky friends. But seriously, she wondered who she'd be sharing the room with.

Alexander placed her on the queen-sized bed, and as soon as her skin met with the fluffy mattress, she relaxed, stretching her body in the process. It was one thing to be carried around and another to move on one's own. She missed being able to do everything all by herself and not having to rely on someone for help. Although some people do fancy being pampered and carried around, she could not imagine her life as a princess.

Despite the friendliness she received on entering, Minnie knew she couldn't let her guard down. She did not trust them, so she couldn't get too comfy, as humans would always be humans.

Cutting into her thoughts, Alexander asked, "So what do I call you? Domi, Minnie, Monique, or Niqué?"

Minnie pressed her lips together. "Just call me by my name, damnit."

He chuckled. "C'mon, Fire, I was only looking at an option of a nickname."

"Geez!" She let out a pronounced sigh. "You don't need to give me a nickname."

Lightening up, he said, "I'm cool with Fire, though."

Ignoring his attitude, she pulled herself up on the bed and faced him. "What the hell am I doing here in this house?" she questioned.

He raised an eyebrow. "What do you mean?" he asked, but immediately, he continued, "I picked you up, took you to the hospital, and brought you here, right?"

She nodded. "Uh-Uh, I get that. But what am I doing here in your home? How long am I to stay here? What do I do in return for squatting with you guys?"

He didn't reply and only sat at the edge of the bed beside her and rested. "This is your home now, Fire, and we're never chasing you away."

Minnie's eyes felt as though they would pop out of their sockets, and she clamped her hands together, alarmed at the fact that he was on the bed with her.

"Why are you on the bed?"

Alex turned to her. "I'm knackered."

"This isn't your room, right?" Minnie spluttered.

On seeing her reaction, he laughed. "C'mon, does this look like a dude's room?"

She scoffed at his playfulness and turned her face from him. He pissed her off and was very unbearable, but this was in a good way. Even if she barely knew him, she could tell that he was only trying to make her warm up to him. But, if only he knew that this was pointless, he'd not try at all.

From her side, he spoke up. "Anyways, this room belongs to Madison."

Minnie turned back to him, wondering who Madison was. However, before she could question this, Alexander stood and walked to the door. "There's a toilet to your left, and it's got a bathroom, too, in case you need to take a shower. Do freshen up, and I'll see you in an hour."

"But…" She tried to object, but Alexander opened the door and walked out.

Minnie faced down, wondering what he meant by one hour and who Madison was. But the door parted open, and Alex peeped in.

"To clarify your thoughts, Fire, don't worry, I'm not lying on the same bed with you," he stated, and a sly smirk crawled up his lips. He added, "For now."

"Asshole!" Minnie cussed as she picked up a pillow, but he closed the door before she could quail it at him. *What a pervert!* she exclaimed, but she couldn't help but laugh at this.

As soon as he left, the silence surged in, and Minnie was drawn into her thoughts. This was the third day after escaping the clutches of Dinah and her past. So far, so good. She was doing great. She just had to go on with her plan to rebuild her life, start anew, and see what would happen.

Hopefully, she'd be able to do that.

* * *

After taking a much-needed bath, Minnie changed into a simple t-shirt and black jeans. Limping out of the room, she supported herself with the walking cane Alexander had left for her. Exploring around, she found herself in the spacious living room, but there was no sign of Alexander, his friends, or Esther. She discovered she missed their annoying selves.

"Are you refreshed?" A feminine voice came from behind her, and this was not Noah's mother. Unlike Esther's, her voice was full of a youthful melodious tone.

Minnie turned, and behind her was a fair-tanned lady. From one look, Minnie guessed they were probably age-mates, or she'd be just a few months older.

"Yes," Minnie replied.

She walked over to Minnie and said, "I guess I haven't introduced myself to you yet." Pulling on a smile, she said, "I'm Madison."

Immediately, Minnie's ears sprang in recollection. Alexander had mentioned her as the owner of the room. This being the case meant she had to be nice to Madison.

With a pulled-on smile, Minnie said, "Nice to meet you, Madison. I'm—"

Madison chimed in, waving her hand rudely, "Yes, I know you, Dominique. But guess what? I do not care."

Minnie's smile fell, and she muttered, "Okay."

Again, Madison intruded with, "You can't stay in my room."

Minnie sighed. "Sure, whatever."

Madison smiled, and she spun towards the room.

Despite her cold attitude, Minnie couldn't give a dime about her. She was about to sigh in relief when Madison spoke up.

"You should know that you aren't welcomed in this house either."

Now, Minnie had about enough of Madison's words. *What does she think of herself?*

She couldn't tell her to leave the house when she wasn't the one who brought her in the first place. Alexander was the only one who could throw her out.

Minnie laughed and strode to Madison, only stopping a few inches from her. Snapping her fingers at Madison, Minnie said, "Missy, I don't give a dime about you and your words, as you can't tell me to leave." She closed in on the surprised girl and continued, "Do you know why? Madison, you were not the one who led me here. So, I will not leave under the influence of your stupid, meaningless words."

Madison's brows furrowed, and Minnie could tell that the poor girl wasn't only shocked and pissed at her. Anyhow, she could not care less.

"How dare you speak to me in that manner?" Madison shrilled.

Minnie chuckled. "Oh, pardon me, your majesty, I had no idea that I had to talk archaic to you," she jested. "Now, shall I take my leave, your majesty?" Minnie added and gave a fake curtsy before walking out on Madison.

With difficulty, she hobbled outside and caught sight of the children playing in circles. On noticing her presence, they stopped and faced her. It was definite that the children didn't like her. Well, the feeling was mutual, as she disliked them too.

"Do you all know where Alexander is?" She threw an open question to the children without expecting a reply. But, much to her surprise, a tiny voice came up from their midst.

"Uncle Dee is at the garage."

Minnie narrowed her eyes, and amid the children stood a little boy of about seven years or thereabout. Sincerely grateful, Minnie grinned and said, "Thanks, kid."

The boy frowned and shook his head. "No, ma'am," he said. "My name is Matthias, and I'm not a kid," he added. "Uncle Oak and Uncle Dee always tell me that I am a man."

Quite against her initial thoughts, children weren't all that bad and could be very helpful as long as Uncle Dee turned out to be Alexander.

"All right, Matthias," Minnie said, and dropping her tone to a whisper, she muttered, "Where is that damned garage?"

On point, Matthias replied, "It's over there, ma'am." He pointed to a small building right down the street.

Minnie flashed the boy a warm smile, turned, and continued down the street, hobbling along the dusty grounds.

Just as the boy had said, Alexander and his gruff buddies were in the garage, working on vehicles.

"Alexander!" she called out, her voice echoing throughout the building and pulling each man out of their work.

Alexander rolled himself from beneath a jeep and stood to face her.

"Took you long enough," he stated and rolled the sleeves of his shirt up to look at an invisible watch. "You're half an hour late."

Minnie snorted. "Half an hour to find you."

Glancing around the garage, Minnie was in awe at the various cars, motorbikes, and other mechanisms surrounding her. Certainly, these men were fascinated by machines.

"Seems you're busy," she commented, and the men laughed.

"Then we'll be busy all our lives," One of the men spoke up.

Minnie shifted her eyes to him, scanning his appearance. He was buffed like Alexander but light-skinned. From one look, she could tell that he was from the eastern parts of the country.

"Josh, here," he introduced himself.

Minnie acknowledged this with a nod.

Beside him, another man also spoke. "I'm Blade."

Minnie threw her eyes at him and raised her brows, surprised. "That's not a real name, right?"

"I don't suppose you know much of names, Fire," Alexander said. "He is Blade Davidson, and that's his biological name."

Minnie chuckled to herself. *Who names their kid after a sharp pointy instrument used most of the time as a weapon?* She wondered what his parents thought when they named him.

"Would you stand there all your life?" Noah asked.

Coming from her thoughts, she saw that the men were all heading out.

"I'll leave when I want to," she answered.

Noah scoffed under his breath and was about to retort when Alexander spoke up. "Oak, we'll join you all in a sec."

Without another word, Noah walked out along with the other two, leaving Alexander and Minnie in the room.

As soon as the men were gone, Minnie looked around, searching for anything else except Alex to stare at. She could feel Alex's eyes boring into her. This was awkward in a good way.

"Hope you aren't starving?"

Ignoring him, Minnie strolled to the nearest car and rested against the bonnet.

Probably used to her snubbing, he laughed.

Minnie expected him to press on, but he just stood there, quiet, as he watched her. She wished she could bring herself to look at him. He wasn't unbearable. He was a definite package of cuteness, and everything around him spelled his handsomeness. His level of hotness was off the radar, and as much as she hated to admit it, she admired him.

Despite this, she couldn't bring herself to trust him, even though all he had done had been nothing but good. She ought to be a bit nicer to him, but she refused to. *Honestly, he ought to stop helping me if he is hoping to get something in return.*

"You know one day you'll eventually drown in the pool of your thoughts," Alex pointed out.

"I'll happily drown in my thoughts than reality," she replied.

He laughed. "Look who is talking. I thought you'd choose a fairytale over your thoughts and imagination."

She rolled her eyes. "There is nothing wrong with imagining perfection, even if it doesn't exist."

He gave a slight nod. "You're right. There's nothing wrong with that."

Satisfied, she grinned.

"Minnie, who are you?" Alex asked.

She frowned and quizzed him, "What kind of a question is that?"

"A question is a question, and it needs an answer," he replied.

Seeing that he was serious, Minnie said, "I'm Dominique, and this is who I am."

He shook his head. "That's not the answer I'm looking for."

She looked at her feet, still frowning. *What does he want me to say?*

Was she to write a five-hundred-word essay just to explain who she was?

"Alexander, what do you want me to say?'"

He sighed, almost in frustration. "What are you? Where do you come from? I need details, Dominique," he said. "I need to know you, the real you."

Snap! He wants to know everything about me. She couldn't just go ahead and confess all her secrets to him. He wouldn't want to know her biography because such a book about her would make parents prohibit their kids from going to the library. The last thing she needed was to refer to her past when her initial plan was to forget all about it.

Making her mind up, Minnie moved towards him, his eyes following her carefully. She stopped inches from him and gazed at him.

Their gazes locked.

She pulled her lips into a bright fake smile. "So, you want to know me, Dominique, the girl behind the attitude?"

His lips curved into a small smile that could be mistaken for a shift at the corners of his lips.

"I wouldn't be asking if I didn't," he replied, his face stone serious.

"Okay, Alexander," Minnie said in her most juicy voice.

She trailed her fingers up his arm, lingering with each touch, and she smirked on seeing the look that crossed his eyes. "As I've said, I am Dominique. I've got no surname," she continued.

She cocked her head to his until their noses were only inches from touching each other. His eyes flashed and dropped to her lips before coming up to meet her eyes, waiting for her reply.

Minnie's smirk deepened, and she said, "Alexander, my story is my info, which means it's confidential, and none of your business."

She turned but did not miss the disappointed look that overshadowed his expectation and the heavy sigh that followed from his downturned lips. This satisfied her. She needed him to stay off her business. Her identity shouldn't concern him or anyone else.

Without another word, Minnie hobbled out of the garage.

Yet, as she continued down the street to the house, she couldn't help but feel dejected at the thought of never getting freed from her past. However, for as long as she could, Minnie promised herself she would keep her past in a tight box, then lock the box in a safe, and bury it under the depth of the earth, and the keys? She'd throw them down to the bottom of the ocean. She didn't want to be Minnie from the past. She wanted to be the newest version of herself. Therefore, she would never risk starting anew by articulating her story to Alexander or anyone else.

* * *

When she arrived at the house, Minnie saw that everyone was gathered around a huge dining table in the backyard. As she walked in, she saw Noah and the other guys who waved her over. Minnie sighed at the sight in front of her, the table settings, and the people seated.

This wasn't her typical dining choice. During her time in the brothel, each girl had to have her meals in her room. They were rarely given a chance to mingle with each other — Dinah ensured they wouldn't. But, on a few occasions, they got lucky and could move around to see each other. However, dining in the open at the brothel was close to impossible.

Minnie ignored their offer and limped away from them, looking for a seat farthest from those she knew, as the last thing she wanted was needless conversation. But, on glancing around, she realized that someone very important was not at the table. *Where on earth is Alexander?*

Instead of receiving his magical appearance, Minnie heard the clatter of chairs, and she looked up to see Madison sliding into the seat by her side. *Oh great, now I have to share seats with my infuriating roommate.*

Seeing that Minnie was on the seat beside hers, Madison groaned and sat down.

Well, as long as they said nothing to each other, Minnie was sure they were going to have a peaceful dinner, but one word and Madison would have it coming for her.

"Let's bow our heads in prayer," Esther, Oak's mother, said, her voice resounding throughout the silence.

Minnie scoffed at this. She hated prayers. *What's the use of hoping and trusting when nothing ends up happening?* Yes, she had never believed in the existence of God. All her principles were based on facts and nothing but realities.

But she had nothing against those who chose to believe in God.

After the prayer, the bowls of food were passed around, but Alexander was still nowhere to be seen. By now, Minnie had begun to worry. What if he had taken her words wrongly and decided to piss off as she had said? If this was the case, then she would continuously have herself to blame. Alexander was unbearable, although it was in a good way. He was sweet and kind, and all he wanted was to know a little bit about her. But she had just shut him up without a single nice thing to say. She shouldn't have, especially not to someone who had been kind and helpful to her.

"Uncle Dee, you're here!"

From her side, Minnie heard Matthias scream. She turned in her seat just in time as Alexander walked to the table and the only vacant seat directly opposite her.

All through the diner, he avoided her eyes and ignored her existence and presence at the table. This confirmed that Alexander was mad at her, and as much as she hated to admit it, she did not want his anger. It's cool if she's the angry one, but not him. She couldn't have the one person who helped her be angry at her. Yes, he was undoubtedly a male and might be a prick at being nice, but he was the sweetest human she'd ever met. This was why she couldn't take his attitude.

***

After the meal, he instantly got up and left the table. Minnie couldn't let him escape. She also stood up and hobbled after him.

He walked into the house, and she tailed him in and only stopped when he hesitated at the entrance to a room.

"Why are you following me, Dominique?" he asked without even looking at her.

Minnie's cheeks felt hot, and she didn't say a thing. Instead, she walked to him, her fingers interlocked.

"Alex?"

He spun to her, a frown etched on his face. "Yes?"

"You literally ignored me all through the dinner, and now you're acting like an ass," she pointed out.

His response to this was just a shrug and the low scoff that followed. She bit the inside of her cheek as he stared at her without saying a thing. *Geez, Alexander is no fun when angry.*

"All right. Is this about what I said at the garage?"

Alex puffed, which sounded like an exasperated sigh, but this was his only reaction.

God, how long do I have to keep up with his attitude? Fine, he wanted to squash her ego. She already did that. He wanted her to apologize. Then she'd do that, reluctantly.

"Alexander, I am sorry."

The corner of his lips twitched into a small smile, and he turned and walked into the room.

Minnie was filled with anger. Did he just walk out on her after she had to apologize —something she rarely did? He couldn't.

She limped into the room, determined to lash him with every word from her lips. But, as soon as she stepped inside, she was swept off her feet and unto the bed.

She instantly tried to shake the attacker off.

On looking up, she saw that it was Alexander, and he had her pinned to the mattress with his arms. The space between them was dangerously close, too close for comfort.

Something flashed in his eyes, and her throat went dry upon realizing what it was. Was he going to force himself on her?

Three

Minnie's heart raced as she stared at him, her eyes frozen open.

"What are you doing?" she demanded.

His lips dissolved into a mischievous smirk, and she became alarmed. Slipping one arm free, Minnie threw her fist to his face, and he instantly rolled off her with a shriek of pain.

"Shit!"

Shooting to her feet, Minnie dashed off the bed, balancing herself on her good foot. She was glad that he was off of her. But, on glancing at him, she winced. *Did I hurt him really bad?*

She moved towards him as a feeling of regret overwhelmed her. She shouldn't have punched him, but he was trying to have his way with her, and this had ticked her off.

"Hey, are you okay?" she asked as she placed her hand on his chin and carefully pulled it to face her.

Well, she had her answer written over his face. She had hurt him really bad. His nose appeared to be broken as he bled.

"I'm so, so sorry, Alexander," she apologized.

Her eyes scanned the room for anything to stop his bleeding, but she didn't see anything she could use. Minnie picked up the hem of the blouse she had on and, without thinking, tore a part of it and used it to apply slight pressure on his nose.

Alexander winced.

Her eyes flew open. She had no idea what to do as she was stomped. Usually, if she hit a man, he'd have to bleed, and she wouldn't be bothered. Actually, she'd be overjoyed and had a victory dance on her bed, waving to her imaginable fans. But this wasn't the case now, as she was terrified.

"What do I do?" She panicked.

What if he bled to death? She couldn't watch him bleed. This would term her cursed if the one person who cared about her ended up bleeding to death.

His warm hand came over her shivering palms, and she immediately looked at his face. There was a slight smile on his lips. Despite his pain and her action, he still found the strength to smile.

"It's alright. I'll be fine," Alexander assured, but she kept trying to hold his blood back with the piece of her blouse.

The material had become dampened with crimson. Minnie's insides twisted on seeing the red that trailed down his nose. She hated blood with a passion.

Alexander gave her palm a slight squeeze causing her to focus on him. In his eyes was pain, but she could sense the calmness in them, and he was asking her to do the same. *But shouldn't it be the other way around?* Shouldn't she be the one to assure him that all would be fine and he wouldn't bleed to death?

"The blood's not stopping, Alex," she stuttered.

However, he squeezed her palm, and she shifted her gaze to him.

"Okay," he began. "There's a First Aid box down the hall."

This was what she needed. She moved out of the room and into the hall. Looking forward, she noticed it hanging on the wall. She hurried to it, using her crutch, and pulled it down. She quickly returned to the room, managing not to place pressure on her ankle.

However, her jaw dropped on seeing Alexander off the bed, and she approached him.

"Dude, you have to be seated!" she exclaimed.

He tried to chuckle but ended up wincing as the pain in his nose surged. "I got bored sitting down," he managed to say.

Minnie placed the box on the bed, opened it, and rummaged through the contents. There were plasters, bandages, gloves, and scissors. Her eyes widened on seeing the wipes, and she exclaimed, "Eureka!"

Alexander laughed, triggering her to look up from the box. "I don't think you'll need that," he pointed out.

Her face fell back to the item in her hands. He might be right, but she didn't have a Ph.D. in curing a bleeding nose. She didn't have a Ph.D. in anything at all.

She placed the wipes back in the container and crossed her arms on her chest, the corners of her lips slightly turned downwards. "So, Mr. Smarty Pants, what do you suppose I use?"

He chuckled. "Well, Ms. Temperance, ice will be okay."

Minnie stared at him in disbelief, unblinking. First, he just insulted her. Secondly, all this while, he knew that ice was all it would take to end his bleeding, but he was just telling her that now.

"You could've told me this minutes ago!" she yelled at him.

Alexander laughed.

Ignoring him, she turned to leave the room in search of ice. The best and the only place she knew the ice was kept was in the kitchen. With this at the back of her mind, she walked to the door.

"Where are you off to?" Alexander asked.

"To get ice," she said as she hobbled toward the door.

Alexander laughed harder.

She spun to him, frowning. "I don't remember dressing as a clown, so what's funny?"

"You are," he admitted with a chuckle. "There's a freezer back there." He pointed towards the farthest end of his room, and lo, there was a small refrigerator.

Her frown cornered into a sneer as she faced him. "So, you knew this, and you're just telling me?"

Not waiting for his derisive reply, she walked to the fridge. She opened it and saw frozen cubes docked in the door of the mini-fridge. She picked one of his nearby clothes, a blue t-shirt, and stocked it with cubes.

Minnie returned to the bed and passed the cube-filled cloth to him, and he placed it over his nose, applying a bit of pressure, while she sat across him, her fingers crossed.

After a while, he removed the already melting ice and cloth with a pronounced sigh. Minnie wasn't sure if the sigh came from her or him, but all that she was certain of was it was a sigh of relief.

Alexander raised his head and met her eyes.

She waited to know how he was, her breaths bated. But he laughed.

"You've got iron fists, Fire, but a cool heart like a petunia," he said.

She sneered at him. "Is that seriously your first comment after you had just survived bleeding to death?"

Instead, he laughed more, which made her even more upset. *Does he have any idea how scared I was?*

She had never had to be so confused, scared, nervous, and uncertain, but he still chose to make a joke out of it.

"Dude, you almost died!" she exclaimed.

Smiling, he answered, "But you, my heroine, saved me."

Minnie sighed. "You're pathetic."

"Oh, but you needed to see how you panicked. I didn't even know you knew how to be scared," he teased.

She gave him a playful swat on his arms. "Idiot!"

He laughed. "Pardon me, Ms. Gasoline."

Enraged, she jumped on him while raining harmless punches, but he laughed as he caught her arms.

"Fire, please do not re-break my nose or re-sprain your ankle," he stated, and they both laughed.

Honestly, he's pathetically stupid, but I'm glad he is all right.

"I'm glad you're okay, Alexander."

"And I'm glad you're here with me," he replied.

She allowed herself to smile while she remained on him, her eyes locked with his. "Thank you."

"Why?"

She laughed. "I haven't said thank you, right?"

He smiled. "Fire, you don't need to thank me. I only did what I had to do," he said.

Minnie felt the corner of her lips quirk into a smile. Strangely, she cared for him, even though he happened to be a male. But he seemed different. Yes. He was an idiot, and she'd never forget he was a male, but she had to own up to herself that he had a way of bringing her out of her zone and making her feel comfortable. As weird as the feeling was, Minnie did not want it gone.

The door to the room banged close, snapping them both out of their moment, and they turned to where Madison stood, her face twisted into a scowl.

"What's going on here?"

* * *

Madison remained in the doorway, frozen with shock. But Minnie climbed off Alexander, as she wasn't ready to fight with Madison.

"What did you think we're doing, Maddie?" Alexander asked.

She only glanced between him and Minnie before laughing.

"Just a stupid incision," she replied and threw Minnie a side glance. "Besides, you couldn't possibly be doing what I was thinking."

Minnie frowned. *What is she trying to imply?*

Madison walked to the bed and sat beside Alexander, snuggling up to him.

Minnie followed Madison's gaze that fell on the blood-stained cloth at the side of the bed. This tipped Madison off, and she eyed the cloth, trailing down to Minnie's ripped blouse, before returning to Alexander's puffed nose. Unable to figure what had happened out, she frowned and faced him.

"What happened to you, Alex?" she asked.

"It's nothing," Alexander answered. "Just that our dearest Dominique felt to test her fists on my face."

Madison's worry was instantly replaced with a glare, and this was directed at Minnie. "You did what?"

"He already explained. You don't need me to repeat, do you?" Minnie jeered.

"How dare you hit him?" Madison shrilled.

"C'mon, Maddie. I know you care about me. You don't need to blow off my hearing to make your point," he said.

She faced him with an apologetic look and pouted. "I wouldn't dare that, Alex."

She squeezed herself under his arm before resting her head on his chest and then using his arm as a drape over her shoulders. "Guess what?" she whispered to him.

Alexander turned his full attention to her.

Minnie knew this was her cue to leave, as she was aware Madison loathed her. "Okay, I'll leave now," she announced.

Both looked at her.

Madison smiled, obviously satisfied. "Bye." She waved. "Do make sure you lock the door on your way out."

However, Alexander kept his gaze on her. "Where are you heading to?" he asked.

Minnie shrugged. She just needed to be out of the room. Madison choked her with her mere presence, and the more she stayed, the closer she got to losing her cool.

"I'm just going to head out," Minnie answered.

"All right," he said and stood, much to Madison's dismay and to Minnie's utmost surprise.

"We're going for a spin," he said. "Care to join?"

Minnie gulped. She wasn't a fan of driving or anything moving fast, but just to irritate Madison, so she agreed. "That sounds like fun, Alex."

Madison's face fell on hearing this, but a bright smile crept up Alexander's face.

"Good. I wouldn't have taken no as an answer," he said. Turning to Madison, he asked, "May we?"

Dejectedly, she answered, "Yes."

"Perfect. Let's go!" he announced and walked out.

Minnie was about to go after him, but Madison beat her to the door, hitting Minnie's shoulder purposely with her arm.

"Oh, I am so sorry, Dominique," she apologized, but even a kid would know that she was being sarcastic.

* * *

Coming out of the building, Minnie noticed the vehicles parked on the road. Many were from the garage, Minnie recalled. Also, Noah and the other guys were hanging around the vehicles.

"You're finally here, Alex," Noah uttered and threw a small wink at Madison. "Hi, Maddie."

She rolled her eyes and looked away.

Ignoring her, he faced Minnie. "You are also here, I see."

"Apparently." She smiled.

Joking, he said, "I thought you were born an indoor baby."

Minnie rolled her eyes at him.

He turned to his brother. "Alex, is she coming with us?"

"She is," Alex replied and glanced at her. "And she'll be my co-girl."

Madison gasped, and the others jeered and hooted, but Minnie just stared at them, completely lost. *What is a co-girl, and why does it feel as though it is a big deal?*

"What's a co-girl?" she questioned Alex, but instead of replying, he simply reached for her hands, clasping them in his, as he walked towards a red convertible.

"You are my co-driver," he finally answered with a laugh.

This sounded amazing, but Minnie wasn't a fan of cars or racing. However, just to spite Madison, she agreed. "Sure thing." She smiled.

Throwing a glance at Madison, Minnie saw that her face had grown red with anger. This was certainly the main deal to Madison, and taking the co-driver seat seemed like snatching candy from a baby.

The others moved to the side of their vehicles, and Alexander did the same.

A long-legged lady walked to the front with a red flag in her hand and a smile on her plump lips.

"Get into your cars!" she ordered.

Everyone got into their vehicles.

Alex turned to Minnie, who hesitated at the car door and pressed the horn twice. "Are you coming, or do we have to wait for another age?"

"Wouldn't hurt, would it?" she replied as she opened the passenger's door and got in.

"Definitely," he muttered, but she ignored him and pulled the seatbelt on.

Looking forward, Minnie saw that the lady held up the flag. "Ready on the left?" she asked.

The cars on the left honked in response.

"Ready on the right?" she asked.

Every car honked, but Alexander didn't. He faced Minnie with a small smile edged at the side of his lips. "Would you do the honors?" he asked.

"Oh, no!" She shook her head.

But he remained adamant.

Seeing that he would not bulge, Minnie sighed. She moved towards him and placed her palm on the wheel. She pushed the wheel, and the loud noise that accompanied this made her jump back. Those horns could shoot up one's blood pressure.

Alexander laughed, and Minnie threw her eyes at him at once.

Chuckling, he said, "You looked funny."

The engines roared to life as Alexander started the car.

"Dominique," he said. "You'll love this," and the car instantly shot off with speed like a light spectrum as soon as the red flag went up.

* * *

After a wild ride through the city, the cars came to rest at the starting point, as all the drivers cheered at the top of their voices to maximize the heat of the moment, while the others celebrated with honking, but Alexander only stared at Minnie.

She was stumped and just stared ahead. She felt her heartbeat racing as if it was going to explode soon while her breath was hitched in her throat.

Minnie was terrified of the speed and his style of driving, but she had to admit it was exciting to get all pumped up. She loved the feeling she got when her heart raced in anxiety, shock, surprise, and fear all at once. This was the true way to live.

"You look fanned out," Alexander commented.

Minnie shook her head, and he laughed. She did not want to admit that she was shaken up, but Alexander had seen through her acts.

"You need to get on the solid ground," he added as he stepped out of the vehicle.

He walked over to her side and opened the door for her, offering his hands for support, but as usual, her ego decided, and she turned him down.

Alighting by herself, she placed her feet on the ground, but the instant she did so, pain shot up her ankle, and she wobbled before she lost her balance and fell into his firm grip.

"Easy there," Alex said as he helped her up. "You seriously need to lie down for a while," he added.

Minnie couldn't argue with this. Despite the fun, racing had made her giddy and nauseous; obviously, this wasn't her thing. Now she had to lie on something comfortable and stable. The last thing she needed was to get on a moving thing.

"I guess you're right," Minnie agreed.

Just then, a teenage girl ran to them, saying, "Dee, a letter came in for you." She caught her breath and continued, "It is from your mom."

Minnie glanced at Alex, surprised that Esther wasn't his mother. Yet, he was the luckiest person in the world, as he had many people who loved and cared for him. This was something she knew she couldn't have. Thus, she envied him. He ought to be happy. However, the distant look he had on his face showed the opposite.

Unable to comprehend his reaction, she narrowed her eyes at him, desperate to understand him.

* * *

The air in the room was timid as Minnie and Alexander sat opposite each other while the others stood at the door, their attention on him. He had his face buried in his palms and was quiet.

Minnie could not wrap her mind around the reason for his attitude towards information from his mother. He did not seem to like the news he received, but he also didn't share this with anyone.

"C'mon, stop brooding like a day-old chick," Noah chided, trying to lighten his mood, but Alexander kept his head down, and the poor guy sighed. "That's it! Dominique, you handle him."

Minnie's eyes went wide, and she was about to object. However, her words hung at the base of her lips as Noah and the others bailed out of the living room. Now, she was left with the mute Alexander. If he hadn't reacted to Noah's witty comment, she could not possibly get him to be full of cheers.

Taking a huge breath, she muttered to herself, "Alright, how do I do this?"

How does anyone make someone who didn't want to be cheered smile? She had no experience with this. She was rather great at making people the opposite of happy. Probably, she could keep her lips sealed and let him work out his issues. However, this would not be fair. She had to help him after all he had done for her.

"Alex?" she called out, but he only mumbled some words, which were incoherently too low for her to catch.

Standing up, she moved to him and sat beside him. "You know I could mistake you for a part of the furniture in this room," she joked, and she heard his cackle.

Seeing that he was loosening up, she continued, "I thought I was messed up, but seeing you now, I'll have to rephrase my words because you look like shit."

He raised his head, and she caught the small smile dangling at the edge of his lips. Whatever she was doing, she knew she had to keep it going, and so, she added, "You are a real pervert, Alexander, getting everyone to worry about your sorry self."

He chuckled and faced her. "You are something else, Minnie."

Proud of herself, she smiled brightly. "Good to have you back, Alexander. I thought I lost you for a while."

He raised an eyebrow at this. "I thought I was a jock who you despise?"

"You still are." She nodded. "But you are that special jock, and I'll not exchange that for a buffed-up Alexander."

He smiled. "Well, I'll take that as a compliment."

"You're allowed to, for now," she said, and he laughed.

"Thank you," he said.

She held up her finger and said, "No, now we are equal. You helped me, and I've returned the favor."

The corner of his lips flipped downwards, and he shook his head. "I'll not like that," he said. "I will find a way to get you indebted to me."

Minnie rolled her eyes. "You can try, but you'll won't."

"Oh." He tilted his head to her. "You bet?"

Smirking, she answered, "How much are you willing to lose?"

"Confident, I see," he pointed out.

She raised her chin. "That's my winning point," she said.

They laughed.

After a while, she faced him with one question on her lips. "By the way, what's with you and your mom—" she began but stopped instantly.

"I'm on good terms with my mom," he replied.

"Uh?"

"I know that's what you were wondering, right?"

Minnie shrugged. "Close to that," she said as she sat on the arm of the chair. "But why does it seem that you don't want to hear from her?" He sighed and said, "I do want to hear from her. She's my mom, after all, and I love her. It is just that—" he trailed off.

"Just what?" Minnie interrupted.

"We just need time away from each other," he said.

A headache quickly ripped through her forehead as she tried to make sense of his words. Why will he need time away from his parents?

Seeing her expression caused him to chuckle, and he continued, "My parents detest my company."

"Whoa!" Minnie exclaimed.

He laughed. "Let's forget about that. I shouldn't have bunked you with my attitude, and definitely, I should not bore you with my sad tales."

"But I'm not—" she tried to object.

Alexander stood up and gently pulled her to her feet without giving her a chance to complete her statement.

"Let's go out to meet the others. The night is near, and we wouldn't want to miss the special moonlight view." He smiled. "This is your first night here. So, it is a must that you see the eighth wonder of the world here in our very own backyard."

"Oh really," she said. "Then, wow me!"

"You bet!" he answered, and without warning, he scooped her into his arms and walked out the door.

* * *

After a spectacular view of the multi-colored sky lit up by the half-moon, everyone retired to their various rooms, including Minnie, who had to go into the same room as Madison.

On getting into the room, Minnie began to remove her excess clothing while Madison applied the cream on her face, which made her look like a clown from the circus.

It had been hours, but neither said a word to the other. This was great. For as long as this went on, then everything would be alright.

Breaking through the peaceful silence, Madison asked, "How do you like the attention Alexander gives you?"

Minnie let out a pronounced sigh. Guess she shouldn't have hoped for peace with Madison around. Pulling on a fake smile, she faced Maddie.

"I love it," she answered.

Madison laughed. "Who wouldn't?"

Cackling, Minnie joined in, "No one."

Then, the silence returned as Madison returned to applying the cream while Minnie fitted herself into a mid-knee gown, comfortable to suffice for a nightie.

"However, you are not going to be any different from the others," Madison spoke up.

Frustrated with her incessant words, Minnie sighed. "Why do you say so, Madison?"

Maddie smiled and walked to Minnie, standing a few feet from her. "It is quite obvious. Alexander has never taken interest in any woman, and you would certainly not be the first," she said and laughed. "However, the others were better looking."

Minnie took in several deep breaths to restrain herself from losing her temper. Madison was only trying to provoke her into saying or doing things she would regret later.

"You aren't dating, are you?" Madison asked.

Minnie followed her breathing techniques, successfully taming the raging fire in her chest.

Madison was bent on breaking through Minnie's control as she continued, "Or, did he pick you up for a one-night stand?"

Minnie shot her eyes at the girl, heat rushing through her veins, and she clenched her fists. Madison was crossing the lines. Yes, she was a prostitute, and she wouldn't deny that, but this was who she was in the past and not who she was now. Madison had no right to judge her and think she was nothing but a sex doll.

Taking her priorities into consideration, Minnie forced herself to remain calm, allowing her emotions to be steady, before calmly saying, "Listen, Madison, I am not here to initiate trouble of any sort." She begged, "I just want to sleep, please."

Madison laughed, her shrill voice breaking through the atmosphere and slashing the serenity in Minnie's head. "Never mind, Alexander wouldn't fancy a thing like you."

This was getting too much for Minnie to bear, but she resumed her calming technique trying to stay focused on positive vibes, although Madison was bent on ripping her walls.

"You're so goddamn ugly that even the bulls would refuse to date you." Madison laughed.

Minnie snapped and flew at Madison, ignoring the pain that ripped through her leg. She gripped Madison's neck, choking the girl.

"How dare you, Madison?"

Madison spluttered, "She wants to kill me. The hideous witch wants to kill me!"

Angered, Minnie pushed Madison off the bed, but Madison was fast to jump back to her feet, and she attacked Minnie with her arms.

"You are a bitch, B-I-T-C-H!" she yelled.

Minnie dragged herself to Madison, pinning her to the wall, but Madison reached for a handful of her hair and tugged hard at it. Minnie released her with a cry of pain as her scalp went up in flame, and her leg felt like it was practically disconnected from the rest of her. She managed to push Madison off, but Madison still held on to her hair.

Instantly, a strong pair of arms pulled her away from Madison. In anger, she turned to hit whoever it was, but her fists hung in the air, realizing that it was Alexander. Tearing her eyes from him, she caught the others watching in the doorway.

"What is wrong with the both of you?" Alexander snapped.

From behind her, Minnie heard shuffling and realized that Madison had stood up. Madison walked toward Alexander, sobbing.

"Alex, she suddenly pounced on me like an animal and began hitting me." She sniffled.

Minnie cackled at Madison's crocodile acts of victimization. She was a liar, a faker, and an attention-seeker. *Well, you've messed with the wrong girl, Madison.*

Alexander pulled his eyes to her, and she forced the huge lump in her throat down on seeing the flare in his eyes.

* * *

"Why would you do that, Dominique?" he questioned, his eyes still seeping with anger.

A sharp pang in her chest ripped through her upon realizing that he had bought Madison's fibs.

"You believe her?" Minnie exclaimed. "Anyone can tell that she's playing the victim now."

He crossed his arms in front of his chest. "Are you the victim?"

Minnie laughed. "No, hell, no. I'm not as pathetic as she is. But neither is this my fault."

Still, under her pretense, Maddie sobbed. "You could have seen how she tried to squeeze the life out of me, Alex. She is so dangerous, and she's capable of killing."

Minnie threw the sadistic pretender a look and scoffed under her breath.

Looking between the two ladies, Alex sighed and said, "Guys, Madison, please leave."

The others at the door exchanged glances, wondering why he suddenly asked them to leave but seeing he was serious, they all begrudgingly walked away from the door.

"You can't seriously ask me to leave you with this murderer, right?" Madison asked.

"Leave, Madison!"

Caught off guard, Madison's forehead wrinkled in surprise, and she gulped. Without another word, she shot Minnie a glare before walking out of the room.

As soon as she was gone, Alexander walked to the side of the room where Minnie had flung her cane, picked it up, and returned it to her.

Minnie collected it, resting her weight on the cane, allowing the pain in her leg to wane gradually.

Silence filled the room for a couple of minutes before Minnie spoke up, frustrated with his silence.

"Look, Alexander, I'm sorry, okay?"

But even this rare show of remorse didn't move him as he stared at her, his gaze hard and intimidating. It wasn't like he was some monster trying to scare the shit out of her, but the silence was too deafening to her.

She needed to hear his voice. She had to know what he was thinking.

"I admit that I went too far with my words and actions, but she began saying all sorts of shits, and I just got tripped off, and well, we all know what happens when I do," Minnie explained.

Alexander remained quiet.

Desperately, Minnie threw her arms up. "Geez, Alexander, I said I'm sorry." She almost yelled. "I didn't mean to hit your girlfriend!"

Then, in an instant, he shot his eyes to her, widening in surprise. "Girlfriend?"

"Yes, she's an ass, but I honestly didn't mean to get into a fight with her," Minnie said apologetically.

The look on Alexander's face remained, and then, he laughed. "You thought Madison was my girlfriend?"

Surprised at his question, she frowned. "It's so damn obvious."

He laughed again. "Oh?"

"Yes." She nodded. "No one gets to hover around a guy that much unless she is his girlfriend."

Alexander raised an eyebrow at this. "Oh, what about a sister?"

Now, it was Dominique's turn to be surprised she pulled her eyebrows up. "She's your sister?"

Without replying, he smiled.

Minnie widened her eyes the more as the realization hit her. Madison wasn't an overprotective and jealous girlfriend. She was his overprotective sister.

"Oh!" Minnie simply exclaimed.

Cutting in with a short laugh, Alex said, "I can't believe that *this* was what started the fight."

Minnie turned to him and crossed her arms in front of her chest. "Now, what are you implying?"

He laughed again, and this pissed her the more.

"C'mon, spill!" she snapped.

Still laughing, he walked to her until he was just an arm-length away from her and cocked his face to hers. In a small whisper, he said, "You were jealous, weren't you?"

Instantly, Minnie chuckled. "Me? Jealous of Madison?"

"Yes," Alex said, a smirk forming on his lips. "Is this correct?"

She laughed. "No, hell, no! I am not jealous of *you* and Madison," she said, emphasizing the word 'you.'

Instead of replying, as Minnie expected, he became quiet and kept looking into her eyes.

Minnie's stomach fluttered when she became aware of how close they were. She felt trapped in her mind as she kept his gaze.

"Why are you suddenly quiet, Alexander?" she asked.

He smiled. "Just admiring you," he said, and his eyes flashed with mischievousness as he added, "And wondering why you like me."

Minnie's eyes snapped open, bemused, and she gave him a playful punch on his shoulders.

"You're a pervert!" She laughed.

He pulled her into a light embrace as he also chuckled.

Her nose scrunched up at the smell of sweat and filth on his body, which was surprisingly pleasant, but she groaned. "You smell like shit."

He laughed. "I love you too."

At that moment, a slight squeak came from the doorway, and Dominique and Alexander faced the door where the others stood eavesdropping on them.

"What's going on?" Oak asked.

Almost immediately, out of the group, one of the guys exclaimed, "It's obvious Alex and Minnie are in a relationship."

An acidic wave welled inside her, and her stomach contracted as their words made their way into her head. Adding to this, Alexander said, "Yes, that is true."

She looked up at him and met his face, a full smirk etched on his lips, and her heart stopped.

A relationship, how did that happen?

Four

Their cheers rang in her ears as she stared at Alexander. Her words knotted in her throat, and she wondered what was happening.

How can we be in a relationship?

For one, she found herself wishing he was for real and he meant his words — that he liked her, but a part of her kept slapping the truth back to her.

He could not have feelings for her.

"Wow!" Oak exclaimed, butting into her thoughts. "Congrats, you two. We need to celebrate this!" he announced.

The others echoed in agreement, all except Madison, who stood to one side, her brows furrowed into a frown.

Alexander laughed. "That is a great suggestion, man." He faced the dumbfounded Minnie and smiled on seeing her expression before asking, "What do you think, Fire?"

His voice finally snapped Minnie back to her surroundings as she threw her eyes to him, then to the crowd at the door, and back at him. With their gaze on her, she felt utterly exposed and suddenly cold. Knowing she could not stay there one more second, she turned and limped towards the doorway, the others parting away to allow her.

Alexander called after her. "Where are you off to, Fire?"

Minnie's chest burned as she walked out the door without replying to Alexander. She could not comprehend his words. She could not be in a relationship with him. No, she shouldn't even consider that.

Brushing off their calls, Minnie found her way out of the building and to the quiet street.

Staring into the space ahead of her, Minnie saw that it was dark and the atmosphere was eerie. It was past midnight — everyone was indoors — everyone but her.

She couldn't stay one more second in the house. She clutched her chest as she felt choked up. It felt like she was locked and cramped up in a tiny space, and she couldn't get out.

Minnie needed to breathe. She needed to disappear. She had to leave.

So, without a second thought, Minnie continued down the lone street.

What did she think when she allowed Alexander to help her? Why did she ever let herself get comfortable with him? She knew what was at risk if she did so, yet she went ahead.

He was a male, and even though he seemed different, he remained a remembrance of the horrible tale of her past. However, she couldn't bring herself to deny him when her whole inside sang a different song.

How could her body which had been hurt by the kinds of his, still crave him?

No, she had to stop this, whatever *this* was.

"Dominique!"

Through the stilled night, she heard her name echoing down the street, and the knot in her stomach returned. She didn't need to turn to know Alexander was behind her.

Under her breath, she begged, "Please stay away from me, Alexander. "

She hoped he'd listen to her, but she knew he would not. Even if he heard her, he would still come after her.

"Please, Dominique, " he called after her.

Her chest burned more on hearing his voice getting closer to her. She took on her heels, dropped the cane, and began to limp faster. She could barely see anything as her tears clogged her eyes.

Fighting against the cold wind of the night that slapped her as she ran, the recollections of her past also threw themselves in her face, reminding her of her place.

"You are a worthless whore, Minnie. See what you've caused again? Alexander should not have to care for you. He shouldn't have anything to do with you. You know this!"

She continued to gait, pushing past her limit and almost stumbling on her bandaged-up ankle, earning her a sharp pang in her leg. She cursed under her breath but did not stop.

"Dominique, please!" Alexander's voice came in closer.

Unable to hold herself, she yelled at him, "Just leave me alone, Alexander, please!"

"Just slow down, Dominique, you'll hurt yourself," he begged, but she shook her head and kept moving farther from him.

No, she could not have these feelings towards him.

She shouldn't care about him. She couldn't trust him. She couldn't like him.

Even though she couldn't see a thing due to the cloudiness in her eyes, she kept strutting as far as she could towards the asphalt road.

She could not think of anything else but run.

A bright light shone on her face blinding her and cutting her short, and she froze as the vehicle moved with great speed towards her. She closed her eyes, expecting the worst, but she was pushed off the lane, and everything blacked out.

* * *

The rays of the sunlight burned through her eyelids, signifying the break of a new day. Minnie peeled her eyes open and was immediately greeted by the blue ceiling above her. She gasped as the events of the previous night poured into her memory.

She bit her lip, recalling how she had run off on Alexander and the family. She also remembered how she was almost squashed by a moving vehicle.

Cocking her head to the side, she saw his eyes gazing at her, and she instantly turned her face away.

She didn't know if she wanted to see his face again after what had happened the previous night. She couldn't tell if she was ashamed of her actions or was simply still trying to run from him.

"I'm glad you're up, Dominique," he said.

But Minnie ignored him, focusing on the decor on the wall.

When she didn't answer, Alexander proceeded, "Why did you run off? You could've hurt yourself."

A stabbing pain ripped through her chest, sensing the sincerity and concern in his voice, but how was she to ascertain and come clean to him that she was terrified of the thought of being in love with him?

"Dominique, if this has anything to do with what I said, then I'm sorry," he said.

Reluctantly, Minnie tore her eyes away from the wall and faced him. "No, Alexander. I believe I've overstayed my welcome here," she stated and pulled herself up to sit.

This caused Alexander's face to contort. He reached for her hand, but she flinched, immediately yanking it back.

"I need to go," she snapped.

He swallowed hard and mumbled, "Where?"

"Anywhere, as long as it isn't here with you," she said and stood, careful not to rest her weight on her ankle.

But Alex wasn't ready to let her go. He reached for her arm and pulled her to face himself. "You don't need to do this, Fire," he cooed.

She shook her head and turned to walk away when her eyes fell on the red bruises on his arms, and she stopped.

Alexander had pushed her away from the road. He had saved her once again.

Her eyes became clouded with tears recalling all he had done for her; how he had helped her when she was helpless, how he had defended her, how he had opened up his home to her, and now, he was offering his heart to her so she could find a place of solace. But she wouldn't dare accept his affection. No, because he deserved someone better, someone purer, someone who wasn't her.

Looking up at him, she sniffed. "Thank you, Alexander, for everything—"

He cut her short. "You don't need to thank me, Minnie."

Minnie stood her ground. "I need to, Alexander. Thanks for helping me, even though you knew nothing about me. Thanks for being there when I needed you. But this is just it. I need to go."

"You don't have to leave, Minnie," he said.

The more he tried to reason with her, the more her heart burned in despair. She wanted him, but she couldn't have him because she had vowed not to have anything to do with his kind.

Why doesn't he just let me leave?

Why doesn't he understand that I'm bad news for him?

"Please, don't make this even harder for me," she pleaded.

"But I'm not, Minnie. I just don't want you to leave," he insisted

She shook herself from his grip. Firming her jaw, she looked at him with all the confidence she could gather and said, "I'm going to be fine, Alexander. I've always managed to survive, and this isn't going to be any different, but you have to understand that I need to leave!"

Alexander's face fell on hearing her words, and he slouched, probably realizing she had her mind made up.

Without another word, Minnie grabbed the cane, picked up her box, and hobbled to the door. She was about to place her hand on the doorknob when he gently gripped her wrist and pulled her back to face him.

Before she could complain, he tilted his face, capturing her lips with his.

All of a sudden, she stopped breathing as his lips met hers. It was as if time had slowed, and for the first time in forever, she didn't think about anything else. She relaxed and allowed him to kindle the flames of passion in her that she never knew she had.

After an eternity of bliss, he released her lips, and their eyes locked.

"I don't want you to leave, Dominique, because I really like you."

She numbed as a sharp tingle rushed across her skin. But she snapped right out of it.

"You don't know what you're saying," she stuttered.

He smiled and tucked a strand of her hair behind her ear. She shuddered when the soft tips of his fingers brushed gently over her skin as he did this.

"I do, Minnie, I do," he breathed the words.

Yet, Minnie shook her head, reminding herself why she shouldn't give in to him, although the more she resisted, the more she yearned to come to the truth with herself. But she couldn't be so selfish to get in with him, so she pulled herself together.

"Alexander, you don't know me. You can't like me!" she yelled, "I'm bad for you, dammit."

"I don't care!"

His voice ripped through the clouds in her head, and all at once, her heartbeat slowed. For the first time, she felt surreal as she stared at him. Those were the words she needed to hear.

He walked to her and held her hands in his own. Bringing his face to hers, he said in a low voice, "I don't care about all that, Minnie. We've all got our pasts and secrets, but all that matters is I admire you, and I'm ready to learn more about you as you do the same with me."

"Give me a chance to care for you, to love you," he added.

Minnie knew she could not keep lying to herself. She was tired of fighting the strong emotions in her heart. She wanted to be with him. She wanted a chance at love. She wanted to be normal for once. She wanted to be free.

So, she stretched to her toes, ignoring the pain spikes in her ankle, and pressed her lips against his as tears streamed down her cheeks. This was it! It was high time she took her freedom into her hands.

Alexander was rigid at first, but he placed his arms on her waist, pulling her even closer to himself.

Minnie wrapped her arms around his neck as their kiss intensified. She could feel the warmth of his skin on hers, and the pounding of his heartbeat assured her of his words as she let herself fall deeper with him.

Never, in her wildest dreams, did she think she'd one day be as helpless as this, and neither did she think of feeling this way about a man.

Slowly, he released her lips and faced her with a small smile.

"Are my feelings requited?" he asked.

She swatted his arm playfully and laughed amidst her sobs, and he smiled.

"C'mon!" She chuckled.

He said, "Just want to hear it from you."

Smiling, she placed her palms on his cheeks and asserted, "I like you too, Alexander. "

"Uh, I didn't get you. Please, come again?"

Without hesitating, she yelled at the top of her voice, "I like you very, very much, Alexander!"

Immediately, he pulled her into a tight embrace and placed a soft kiss on her forehead while keeping his arms securely around her.

* * *

As soon as the whole house knew that she and Alexander were dating, things took a wild turn. Of course, they instantly knew because they were eavesdropping on them, as usual.

Everyone seemed cool with this new information. Even Madison seemed not to mind, not that she had a choice.

Minnie's relationship with Madison remained the same, however. Although dating her brother, Minnie had to converse with Madison. However rare it might be.

The following week, Alexander received news from his mother about a tournament hosted by Canaan Motors, and he needed to be a part of it. This prompted Minnie's curiosity to learn more about his family.

This time around, Alexander did not hesitate to tell her about the popular Canaan family. His grandparents had ventured into manufacturing vehicles during their youth days. His father, engineer Matthew Canaan continued in their footsteps. He further enhanced the business by creating the annual "Race for All It's Worth" competition which featured the best race drivers from all over Africa, including Alexander and his twin brother, Andrew J. Canaan.

Minnie was surprised when he told her he had an identical twin, and from the others, she found that all the brothers shared were their looks and had nothing else in common, as they could barely stand each other.

Alexander further revealed that Madison was his cousin. She was the daughter of his father's brother, but his parents adopted her when her mother died after just giving birth to her. However, Madison was never treated as just a cousin.

This revelation explained a lot about Madison's attitude, and at once, Minnie forgave the poor girl.

Then, Alexander told her that he had left home with Madison when his father clarified that he would have to participate in the fanciful competitions, and Alexander disliked this as he never fitted into the place, and thus, he never raced. So, he left the easy way and came to the ghetto, where he could experience life on the wheels from the raw perspective — the true way of racing. However, he and Madison had become attached to Noah and his family, and they had remained with them ever since.

***

Everything was normal for weeks until one day, Alexander and Minnie had just returned from the hospital, where the final checkup was done on Minnie's ankle and her bandage removed. Luckily, her ankle injury healed, and she was free to use her leg again. Not too long after settling in, they were informed by one of the kids that a messenger from the Canaan Estate was at the entrance with a message from his mother, Dr. Abigail Canaan.

"What message do you bring, Simon?" Alexander asked.

"Sir, your mom, has requested your presence at the estate," the man answered.

Alexandra's brows became raised, "Is everything alright there?" he asked again.

The messenger looked down, avoiding his eyes.

The corner of his lips became downturned, and he narrowed his eyes at the man. "C'mon, speak up, Simon."

Immediately, Simon looked up and said, "Your father is ill."

Alexander stiffened at this news, but Minnie squeezed his palm. He glanced at her, and she smiled to let him know everything would be just fine. This seemed to work as he returned his eyes to the messenger.

"Tell mom I'll be there in two days."

With this, the messenger bowed and left.

"Why two days?" Minnie turned to ask him.

"I do have to get back home," he said.

"You have to, but why not leave now?" she asked.

He smiled. "Fire, it's not that easy to prepare two ladies instantly when one is a ball of attitude, and the other is brimstones of fire."

Minnie laughed and gave him a playful punch, knowing exactly what he meant, but then a prickling sensation shot up her spine. *What will his parents think of me?*

Alexander must've seen the uneasiness in her and held her hands in his. "Hey, are you okay?" he asked.

She forced on a smile. "Yes, I am."

This seemed to satisfy Alexander. He leaned in, placing a kiss on her forehead.

* * *

"I still can't believe you are leaving already." Esther sobbed. "I mean, I've already gotten used to seeing the three of you here."

"C'mon, we'll be back before you know it," Alexander cooed.

A small smile stretched her lips as she nodded and faced Minnie and Madison. "You both take good care of him." She threw a wink at Minnie. "Most especially you."

Minnie threw a side glance at Alexander before returning to the lady with a smile and saying, "I will.

Noah chimed in, "You must keep me updated, Alex."

"Will do." Alexander nodded.

"Alright, be on your way now," Esther spoke up, playfully shoving the three towards Alex's jeep. "You have a long journey ahead, and I don't want you traveling in the dark, okay?"

"Yes, ma'am." Alex laughed and got into the jeep, Minnie following into the passenger side while the quiet Madison filed into the back.

Then, ripping through the silence of the evening, a sharp cry resounded from the house, and everyone turned their attention to the little child heading to the jeep. Alex instantly jumped out and crouched to scoop Matthias into his arms.

"Why are you leaving me, Uncle Dee?" The boy sobbed.

"No, kiddo, you know I can't leave you," Alex said, trying to soothe the boy, whose lips remained pulled down.

"But you are leaving, aren't you?" he insisted.

Minnie smiled as she saw the plea in Alexander's eyes when he turned to them for help. Against her initial judgment of children, Minnie, through her weeks in the house, had come to like the little devils who had warmed up to her and tried their best to get her to become their play buddy. However, her favorite among the children was Matthias, who was always looking to keep her preoccupied with his wild curiosity and many questions.

Minnie had learned from Esther that Matthias was the heritage of her first son, Jonathan, a navy sub-lieutenant, who had died fighting for the nation when Matthias was a toddler. Esther further explained that Matthias's mother had passed away during his birth. But none of this had ever affected the seven-year-old, loved by everyone and adopted by Noah and Alex.

So, she understood how close Alexander had been to Matthias, and she knew she had to convince the boy that his uncle wasn't going anywhere for long.

"Matt," she called to the boy, who threw his innocent eyes at her. "You know what? I promise you we won't be away for too long, and we'll get ice cream and chocolate for you and your friends."

This seemed to work. Matthias' already enormous eyes widened the more.

"Really?" he asked.

Minnie nodded with a bright smile.

Matthias wiped his face with the back of his hand and pulled into a cheerful smile.

Sniffling, he said, "Uncle Dee, please get me a strawberry and vanilla-flavored ice cream."

"Alright, boss," Alex said, and Matthias wrapped his arms around his neck. "Take care of Uncle Oak and grandma, okay."

"Aye, Captain!" The boy giggled and climbed down from Alex.

Instantly, Alex sighed and said, "Now that's settled. Let's be on our way."

"Before he changes his mind," Esther pointed out.

They all waved on as Alex reversed from the street and then drove forward until the slums disappeared behind them, and the asphalt road came into sight.

Glancing at the rear mirror, Minnie noticed and watched Madison as she busily scrolled through her phone, her eyes fixated on it.

"This is boring," Alexander spoke up, breaking the silence in the car. "Some music?"

"Sure," Minnie agreed.

Madison disagreed, saying, "Please, don't."

Instantly, the idea was shoved out of the window, and the journey was continued in silence, everyone preoccupied with their thoughts.

Even though Minnie tried to remain calm, it was hard as she kept wondering what the rest of his family was like and whether they would be more like Alex or like Madison.

But, most importantly, if they would accept her as his girlfriend.

* * *

After several minutes of driving in total silence, Alexander brought them to the front of a huge black gate and honked twice. At the second honk, the gates were pulled open by two men dressed in military uniforms.

Minnie's heart hammered against the hard of her chest, and her head began to ache as the uncertainties ahead slowly overwhelmed her.

Driving in, Alexander parked under the garage shed. Immediately, Madison stepped out, strolling into the mansion. He turned to Minnie, who couldn't relax her closed-in expression. He placed his palm over hers that rested on the armrest, snapping Minnie's attention to him.

As if reading the anxiety off her face, Alexander leaned towards Minnie and cupped her cheek in his palms, bringing her attention to him.

"They aren't monsters, you know?" he joked.

She snarled at him. "Alex!"

He assured, saying, "I'll be with you the entire time."

Somehow, this brought the ravaging emotions in her to slowly quieten, and she smiled.

Taking a huge breath, she firmed up, opened the car door, and stepped out. Following her, Alex also got down, and they walked into the magnificent house.

When she entered, Minnie gawked at the beautiful arrangement of the interior decors. Her wandering eyes fell on a slightly rounded woman seated on a sofa in the room.

She was beautiful, and Minnie didn't need to be introduced to her to know she was Dr. Abigail Canaan, Alexander's mother.

"Mom," Alexander confirmed this as he walked towards the woman who kept her glance at the three, her eyes fixated on the strange lady amid her children.

Returning her eyes to her son, she frowned. "If I hadn't requested to see you, would you have come, Alexander Canaan?"

"My apologies, Mom." Alexander smiled.

Immediately, the woman's lips stretched into a big smile, and she scooped him into a tight hug, and Alexander wrapped his arms around her.

"I've missed you, my baby boy," she sang.

Unable to resist this cuteness, Minnie smiled even though her heart bled at the thought that she had never had anyone care or love for her like a mother would do, and at once, she wished her mother was with her.

Slowly, the mother released her son and turned to Madison, who was busy purposely typing away on her phone.

"*Madison* Andrea Canaan." She stressed Madison's name, causing the girl to reluctantly peel her eyes off her phone. Frowning, she asked, "What do you have to say for yourself, young lady?"

Madison rolled her eyes and lazily said, "Hello, Mom."

The woman shook her head. "No. Would you throw that attitude away and come hug me?"

Full of grumbles, Madison walked to her and draped her arms around the woman. Unsatisfied with this, the woman pulled Madison to herself, enveloping the girl in a bear-crushing hug, causing Madison to cough.

"C'mon, Mom!" Madison complained.

Laughing, Alexander butted in, "You'll squeeze the life out of her, Mom. You know she hates hugs."

Reluctantly, she released Madison, saying, "Well, she has to love mine."

Then, she turned her attention to Minnie at once.

"Alex, would you care to introduce her to me, or would you prefer my imagination to run wild?" she asked.

Without allowing Alexander to speak, Minnie said with a smile, "Hello, Dr. Canaan."

The woman pursed her lips and took a few calculated steps towards Minnie.

Minnie could feel her heart beating against her ribcage as the woman's eyes bore through her. She was scared she would dislike her and tell her to leave Alexander.

To Minnie's shock, Dr. Canaan's lips pulled into a bright smile, and she enveloped Minnie in a warm hug.

Then, bursting through the air, she said, "Lovely meeting you, daughter-in-law."

Minnie's breath clogged in her throat, causing her to cough.

Daughter-in-law?

Five

Madison laughed, breaking through Minnie's frozen state, and Alexander chuckled.

"C'mon, Mom!" He laughed. "Let me handle the introductions, will you?"

Reluctantly, Alex's mom released Minnie from the hug, and once again, Minnie could breathe freely. However, Minnie couldn't deny that she loved the feeling of being wrapped in a warm embrace, which signified motherly love, care, and affection. At once, her skin pores began yearning for another hug, but Minnie slapped this back as soon as she recalled what the woman had called her.

Daughter-in-law.

"I know you'll not admit this, my baby boy, but my old eyes can't deceive me," Dr. Canaan said.

Laughing, Alex said, "You're not old, Mom."

She smiled in appreciation. "I am not. I am still a beautiful teenager. "

Madison scoffed. "Yeah, at fifty."

Abigail folded her arms in front of her chest; her lips pulled downward. "Are you jealous of me, young lady?"

"Yeah, right," Madison sarcastically said before striding through the house.

His mother turned to Alexander, nodding him to proceed. He smiled and glanced at Minnie beside him before facing his mother again.

"Well, Mom," he said. "This is Dominique, my girlfriend." Returning to Minnie, he added, "Dominique, this is my mother, Dr. Abigail Canaan."

Minnie's heart warmed upon seeing the approving smile that the woman had on. She smiled, saying, "Nice to meet you, Dr. Canaan."

Dr. Canaan's face brightened. "Call me Abigail, sweetie." She then added, "You've got a beautiful name, Dominique. What is your surname?"

Minnie's bowels flipped. She went blank instantly. How could she assert to this woman that she had no parents, no roots, and, therefore, couldn't possibly have a surname?

Luckily for her, Alex stepped in. "We'll attend to formalities later, Mom."

The woman's eyes remained on Minnie, increasing the flutters in her stomach.

Luckily, she tore her eyes from Minnie, turning to her son.

"Alright, Alex. You owe me an explanation," Abigail agreed.

Changing the topic, Alex asked, "Mom, how is dad?"

It was clear from his tone that he was concerned, even if he tried to act as if news of his father's ailment hadn't affected him. His question hung in the air, and Abigail's smile disappeared.

"He is much stable now," She answered, and the lines on Alexander's face smoothened. Adding in, she said, "Come with me." and progressed deeper into the house.

Alex turned to follow his mother when he hesitated and turned to Minnie.

"Let's go, Minnie." He gestured to her.

"Do I have to?" she asked in a low voice.

Alex cocked his face to her and said, "Only if you'll care to join Madison in her room."

Minnie sighed. "I can stay here, can't I?"

"Nope." He smiled.

"C'mon, Alexander and Dominique," Abigail called from inside the house.

"So, shall we?" Alex asked.

Defeated, Minnie said, "Alright."

Alex smiled and clasped her hand with his before they proceeded into the house together.

* * *

Abigail stopped at the entrance to a double-panel door on the last floor of the mansion. She turned to Alex and Minnie with a smile before sliding the door open and walking in.

From a glance, Minnie noticed a man lying on a traditional canopy bed, the ones she had seen in movies she had watched with the girls back at the brothel. Her eyes further wandered about the room, admiring the beautiful decor, which was uniformed in silver and purple. Minnie's eyes fell back on the man, and she noticed he was awake but weak.

However, his thick lips pulled into a small smile on seeing his son.

"Alex," he called.

Alexander walked to the bed and was soon at the side of the bed, cupping his father's hands in his own.

"How are you holding up, Dad?"

"I'm living, despite my sons deserting me," he answered.

"I'm here now, Dad."

Smiling, the man pulled his hand free from Alex's grip and raised it to the side of his son's face. His eyes read his son with keen interest.

"It feels good seeing you again," the man said.

His eyes wandered from his son and fell on the strange girl standing at the doorway, a small frown forming on his forehead.

Alex followed his father's gaze, and his eyes fell on the person of his father's attention: Minnie.

"Dad, meet Dominique," Alexander spoke up, but his father kept his focus on Minnie.

Continuing, Alexander added, "She is my girlfriend."

Minnie gulped. Why did Alex have to be so blunt and truthful? She knew the man would not accept that his son had someone like her as a girlfriend.

The look of displeasure on his father's face grew as he scrutinized Minnie. Minnie felt his eyes bore into her, and her heart dropped. *He did not like me.*

Just as she had presumed, Engineer Canaan spun his eyes to his son, his lips curling into a sneer. "I see," he began. "Not only did you choose to mingle with those vagabonds, Alexander, but you've also chosen to dirt yourself with one of their kind."

His words exploded right in Minnie's face, tearing and ripping her mind into shreds, and she froze.

"Matthew!" Abigail chimed in.

"Listen, young woman," Matthew continued, his eyes on Minnie. "Alexander is of royal blood. He is a Canaan, and someone like you cannot dream of ever being with him. Is that understood?"

He was about to continue his hurtful words and abuses, but Alexander cut him off.

"We would take our leave now, Dad," Alex said, standing from the side of the bed.

He walked to Minnie and clasped her hand in his.

Matthew's frown dissolved as his expression dampened.

"But you just got here, son," he stuttered.

Instead of replying to his father, Alex turned to Abigail, saying, "We'll see you both in the morning, Mom."

With this, he tugged Minnie, who, although still stumped, took his cue to leave, and both walked out of the room, down the stairs, and were about to head out when Abigail called from the top of the staircase.

"Alexander! Dominique! Please, wait up!"

Hearing this, Minnie and Alex stopped at the door and watched as she hurried down the stairs to them.

"Mom," Alex said, but Abigail let out a faint smile, cutting him short.

"It's alright, son. I will talk to your father."

Alex nodded. "Thanks, Mom."

She sighed and faced Minnie. "Please forgive his words, child. He barely meant any."

Minnie forced a smile on and said, "Sure. I understand."

"Thank you, Dominique." She threw her eyes back at her son. "It's late. Where are you both heading to?"

"The Ardor House," Alex answered.

"Alright, be safe." Abigail smiled.

Alex returned the smile, and he and Minnie turned to the door, walked out of the house to his car, and got in.

Alex drove out of the premises. As the house disappeared into the distance, Minnie looked in the rear mirror and sighed. That didn't go as planned, but was she surprised? No. However, she had let in a speck of hope, but now, reality had slapped back on.

* * *

The car was as silent as a graveyard as Alex drove through the streets of Lagos, his focus on the road but his mind lost in the world of his thoughts. Minnie looked through the window, watching the road speed beneath the car as her thoughts roamed her mind.

The road stretched for miles, causing her to wonder if the ride would ever end. The more the car moved, the more she questioned their destination. She did not know where they were or where they were heading. All she could see were the tall savannah trees by the sides of the road, which greeted them with the cool whispers of the evening air.

Minnie knew they were far from the Canaan mansion.

Then, Alex took a turn onto a bare road heading into the thickest of the shrubs, and at once, she worried.

She did trust him. She truly did. Yes, she might not know him as well as he didn't know her, but she was certain that she could not fear him, and neither could she doubt his actions or his love. Though it was the most normal thing to question where he was driving to, her lips were glued together as his father's words resounded in her ears.

"Not only did you choose to mingle with those vagabonds, Alexander, but you've also chosen to dirt yourself with one of their kind."

Engineer Canaan was right about one thing. She was a vagabond, but if only he knew her, then Minnie could imagine his words and actions. Yet, she had hoped he'd not judge her without getting to know who she was trying to become. However, the plain truth was Matthew had rejected her.

How could she have considered getting accepted by his family?

Maybe his mother had accepted, but reality had just confirmed that her dreams had clouded reality. She should have done none of this. She shouldn't have hoped for the impossible or allowed Alexander to get deep with her.

She cared for Alexander. She truly did. But he did not deserve to be stuck with filth like herself. He had a good heart and deserved nothing but innocence.

Unfortunately, she was neither.

"Minnie?" Alex called her out of her thoughts.

His voice ripped through her clogged mind, and she looked away from the window. His forehead flopped in worry, and he narrowed his eyes at her.

"Are you alright, Fire?"

Pulling up a fake smile, Minnie answered, "I'm perfectly fine, Alex. It's not a new thing to be denied by the father of your boyfriend without being given a chance to prove yourself, is it? It's great. I'm great. *Everything's great.*" She mumbled the last part. Her chest felt hollow. It was as if Matthew's words were clogging her heart.

She noticed Alex's eyes on her drooped at their edges, and he pressed his lips into a thin line. He reached for her palm with his free hand, giving it a warm squeeze.

"I'm here for you," he said, and Minnie nodded, all her thoughts clouding her mind as he kept driving on.

After some minutes, Alexander brought the car to a halt, and Minnie looked to the front and noticed a small bungalow in the cluster of trees. It was slightly dark, but she could still see the creamy-colored walls.

The birds in the trees welcomed them with their harmonious songs and rhythmic beats that were accompanied by the flaps of their wings. The beautiful moonlight enhanced all this as she spread her wings over the house, standing proudly in the sky, screaming blissfulness.

The night was perfect, inviting her to embrace the nuttiness and wildness, but there she was, trapped in her emotions.

Tuning these out, Minnie glanced at Alex and asked, "What's this place?"

The corners of his lips shifted upwards, but that was the closest to a smile he had on.

"This is the Ardor House," he answered. "Our holiday home."

Minnie felt her heart flip at this as the imagination of being with him and sharing a holiday home as true lovers flashed in her mind, but this died off as reality ushered itself back.

"C'mon," she said as she opened the door and jumped out of the car before Alex could notice the tears that gathered in the curves of her eyes.

She hastened her steps to the bamboo structure that made up the gate of the Ardor House, trying to get farthest from him.

Behind her, she heard the car door lock, and she knew that Alex had also stepped out of the car. She kept her face at the gate, biting back the strong urge to break down as the choking hold on her heart was getting too overwhelming.

Yet, she almost jumped out of her skin when his brawny arms gripped her from behind, but as soon as the sweet smell of his cologne hit her nostrils, she relaxed to his hard front. His warm breath came over her neck. "Planning on hosting a crying party without me?"

Sniffling, she turned in his arms until she faced him and mouthed, "No."

His lips drew into a smile, and he placed his head on her shoulder, burying his face in the side of her neck. Minnie's chest warmed, feeling his cuddle as a warm blanket wrapping her racing heart.

Whispering to her, he said, "Dominique, I'm sorry."

The thing she couldn't accept was him taking the blame. It wasn't his fault that his father was blunt and slightly overprotective of him. Neither could she blame Matthew, as he only did what parental instincts urged him to do.

"Why are you apologizing?" she asked.

He drew in a long breath before answering, "Minnie, I shouldn't have taken you there." He paused, burying his nose in her hair. "I know my dad. I knew what he could do and say, yet I made you go through that."

Minnie wrapped her arms around him as she could not think of a word to say. All she wanted was to feel him beside her. She needed to be assured he'd never disappear. She wanted an assurance, however little it might be, that Alex would always be hers, come what may.

"Are you both intending to stay outside forever?"

A woman's voice came from the house, and they looked to see an elderly woman standing behind the bamboo gate.

"Nana!" Alexander exclaimed, and the woman's lips stretched into a huge grin as she opened her arms, inviting him for a hug. Smiling, Alex walked into her outstretched arms, and she wrapped him in a cuddle.

"Jose, where have you been all this while?"

Minnie smiled at the revelation that Alex's initial was Jose, Alexander Jose Canaan.

"I'm here now, aren't I, Nana?" Alex laughed.

The woman scoffed. "Eventually, yes."

Leaving the hug, she faced Minnie, her eyes dancing over her, and the smile on her wrinkled face reappeared. "Who are you, my dear child?"

Minnie threw a glance at Alexander, and he gave the nod to go on.

"I'm Dominique," she introduced herself.

The woman walked toward Minnie and stopped a few inches from her. "You are really a Dominique," she said.

Minnie's brows curved at this as she wondered what the woman meant.

As if reading her mind, the woman came closer to Minnie and cupped her cheeks in her frail hands. "You are beautiful, and you've got a strong heart." Her smile widened, and she added, "Just like Dominion."

Minnie gawked.

Who is Dominion? she questioned herself.

Two arms wrapped around her waist, holding her from behind, and she relaxed, knowing it was Alexander. Confirming this, he spoke up from her back.

"Nana, we are tired. We'll chat tomorrow, okay?" he suggested.

Nana smiled. "Oh, definitely, my dear Jose."

She turned to the building, walking in, and the duo followed her, both taking in the house ahead of them.

The Ardor House was fairly decorated. From what Alexander had said, it had been there for several years, but it maintained its beauty and importance. Minnie noticed an old playground at the farthest end of the yard. It looked like it had served the purpose of its installment, and now, though redundant, it still symbolized a garden of love, cheerfulness, happiness, and a reminder of childhood. These things had been missing in her childhood. Things she would never have.

Sniffing back a tear, Minnie recalled the memories of her childhood. It was always her and the girls. Several girls, she had grown a liking for, but this was always for a short while, as they would suddenly disappear when she had thought she had found a friend.

Now that she thought of it, she never really had a friend. There was no one to confide in. She never really had anyone to rely upon. She had no one she could trust.

However, Alexander had awakened all this in her, and she wished she would never have to return to the tale of the former times.

Never again, she prayed.

* * *

Despite their pleas to rest, Nana insisted on giving the duo a tour of her grand home, including the grounds, even as Minnie and Alex yawned at different times during their walk.

This, not being enough compensation for leaving her, Nana made the duo sit for tea with her, and she filled their ears with tales of the childhood days of Alex, and his twin brother, Andrew, when they came for holidays with her, and her late husband, Dominion.

She further spoke of how her late husband took delight in becoming the boys' playmate each time they came to visit from the states. Moving on, she spoke of how the boys grew distant from her after her husband died.

However, saving them from further earfuls, Nana had to retire to bed because of her condition, which required her to be in bed before she triggered heart failure.

Finally, it was just Minnie and Alex, and this was time to speak about the incident with his father. However, Minnie was reluctant to bring that up, so she diverted her questions.

"How was your grandfather to you?" she asked as she watched Alex tidy the bed in the room Nana had prepared for his parents when they came to visit. Although no one had used the room for a while, it looked neat and smelt fresh. Nana was a clean lady.

Alex raised a brow at her question. "What do you mean?" he countered.

"Well…" She trailed off as she tried to picture a younger Alex with his grandfather before continuing, "How was your relationship with him? Both you and your twin."

Alex smiled. "Granddad was the best," he began as his smile stretched brighter, and his eyes glistened when he stared into the space. "He was my mentor, talk buddy, and best friend. When he was around, we were thrilled. There were no fights he couldn't handle, as he preached peace to everyone around him."

He brought his eyes back to her and added, "He was the best grandfather any grandson could have."

Minnie's eyes moistened at the thought of her having a grandfather, too, but she waved this off with a smile. "Seems you had a colorful past with him."

His eyes sparkled as he answered, "Oh, we all did."

Taking the beauty of the moment, Minnie walked to him and wrapped her arms around his waist, and he pulled her closer to himself.

"Dominique, be truthful. Are you alright?" he asked again.

Her smile fell as she recalled the realities surrounding her, each echoing the fact that she was a desolate girl roaming around the world without no true cause. Maybe, truly, she was a vagabond.

"Dominique—" He tried to speak, but Minnie was quick to interrupt as she pulled her face to him.

"It's alright, Alex. I'm good, honestly."

He stared at her for a while before bringing his palms to the sides of her face. He leaned into her until what was left between them was too close to be called space, and he whispered, "I love you, Dominique."

Without doubt, she knew he meant it, and she also asserted, saying, "I love you too, Alexander."

His cheeks dimpled as he angled his lips over hers, capturing her soft, luscious lips with his, parting them with a slight force.

Minnie closed her eyes, letting herself drown in the passion between them. This was an amazing feeling, one she never thought she'd feel. She was there, in the arms of a man she loved, sharing her truest kisses, her heart, and her love with him.

However, Alex broke out of the kiss, saying, "We need to get some rest, Minnie, before Nana comes bothering us again."

Yet Minnie was left wanting more. The sensation of his lips on her lingered a little longer than expected, and she had to get more from where it came from.

Swiftly, she grasped his hand, and he turned to her, his brows raised. Before he could react, Minnie crashed her lips on his. Despite his surprise at her move, he placed his hands on her hips, pulling her closer to himself. Deepening the kiss, she laced her fingers through his hair.

She loved him. She wanted him. She desired him. She needed him.

Releasing his lips, she was met with his desire-filled eyes, and he rolled his tongue over his lips, relishing the taste of her kiss.

"Are you aware of what you are starting, Fire?" he mouthed.

Without hesitating, Minnie said, "I don't know if you are quite ready for this, Alexander Jose Canaan."

His lips pulled into a stylish smirk as he cocked his face to hers, keeping their gaze straight. "Bring it on," he breathed.

Satisfied, Minnie smiled. She traced a finger along his jawline, down to his chin, and gently tilted his head to hers before taking his lips with hers again. His hands tightened around her, and she pressed deeper into him, heightening their kiss.

"You know I've been a good boy, but you are just that bad girl, aren't you, Fire?" he teased as he trailed kisses down her neck slowly.

Minnie moaned. "Seems I've won, and you lose."

Alex chuckled into her skin. "Uh-Uh, I never lose," he said. "I only win."

"Oh," Minnie smiled. "We will see what happens."

A coy smile flashed across his face, and he said, "Surely we will."

He immediately returned his lips to hers.

Minnie felt his fingers slide into her hair, pulling her closer to him. She could feel the warmth of his skin and the pounding of his heartbeat as she wrapped her arms around his neck.

"We could stop this now," Alex muttered, though Minnie could tell that he did not mean it and she wasn't planning on ending what she had started.

Pulling her lips to his ear, she whispered, "Don't. You. Dare."

He laughed once. "As her majesty wishes."

In an instant, he swept her off her feet, taking her unawares, but she was quick to wrap her legs around his waist, lacing her arms around the strong towers of his neck. She silently hummed as she felt the firm muscles of his arms flex when he carried her and placed her on the bed.

She leaned against the bed wall as he brought himself over her.

His eyes met with hers, and he smiled. "How did I get so lucky to have you?"

"Alex," she mouthed. "I ask myself that too."

Without giving him a chance to speak, she trailed her hands down the muscles of his back, earning a groan from him. He moved to her, pressing her even more to the bed, and hungrily his lips came down on hers. His hands wandered to her chest, trailing down, exploring every inch of her, yet lingering on each spot that caused her to gasp. His fingers hesitated, and her shirt buttons flew open, revealing her bare skin and her breast anchored in her lace bra.

"God, you're so beautiful, Minnie." He breathed.

Minnie moaned when she felt his breath hot on her skin as he kissed down her neck to her chest.

She leaned into his touch and the sizzling sensation of his lips on her skin. She bit down a moan as he nuzzled her collar, his hands moving in perfect circles around her bare stomach.

Alexander brought his mouth to her earlobes, and there was heat in his voice as he asked, "Minnie, are you sure of this?"

Minnie had no reason to hesitate because she was surest of the languages emanating from her heart, and although alien to her, she could not refuse their calls.

"I am," she answered, "Are you?"

He nibbled on her earlobes, and she giggled. He brought his eyes back to hers, and with all determination, he said, "I want you, Minnie."

Minnie smiled as her heart flipped in excitement. She wrapped her legs around his waist as he braced himself against the bed with one hand. Slowly, he began rocking his hips with hers, and she felt the hardness in his trousers. Her hands swept past his mound as she pulled his zipper open.

Alex pulled her closer as if the space between them was wider than all oceans combined. He continued rocking his hips with hers, and she gasped in pleasure. Instinctively, she clutched at his back, drilling her nails into his skin, earning a moan from Alex as she pulled him to herself with each shift of his hips.

Unable to hold herself, she called out. "Oh, Alex!"

Her back arched against the bed as they found a rhythm together till all between them was a perfect symphony. All she could feel was the drive of their bodies and the sweet ecstasy budding between them.

"C'mon, Fire!" Alex groaned.

Minnie could feel herself nearing her climax, and with a wild scream of pleasure, she cried, "Oh My God!"

Six

After a while, they lay together with Minnie's head on Alexander's chest and his arms draped warmly around her – unclad under the covers and happily breathless. He picked her hand up and playfully laced his fingers with hers, interlocking them gently, and Minnie smiled to herself.

She could barely comprehend that she was lying in bed with a man she loved. Usually, all those who lay with her were her clients, but Alexander was different, and this moment with him was exceptional and truly special.

"Minnie." He called her out of her thoughts. She pulled herself to his face until she stared him in the eyes.

"Hey," she said.

Using his other hand, he trailed a finger over her lips, his eyes glancing fixated on them before looking back at her. "I never want to lose you," he said.

Minnie's heart skipped a beat, a weird coldness shooting through her.

Before she could speak, he asked, "I hope you would never leave, Minnie?" The feeling in her insides grew more acidic as she kept her eyes locked with his, trying to read his emotions of him. "I hope I can always trust you. I hope you will grant us the chance to get to know each other better and truly."

The more the words left his lips, the more she kept drawing herself into her cage of thoughts. How could she promise to be with him when she wasn't even sure of what she would do next? How could he trust her when she didn't trust herself? How could he get to know her when she had sworn never to speak of her past to anyone, including him?

"Promise me, Dominique, that I can always count on you." He paused, keeping his gaze locked with hers. "Promise me I can always lean on you."

At this, Minnie blanked.

Was it fear stopping her from promising him? Or was she insecure?

She could not tell, but she knew she wouldn't be able to bear it if he left her. So, yes, she was scared. Yes, she was insecure. She knew that as long as she kept her past from him, she couldn't possibly be happy with him. Yet, she wouldn't tell him because she was sure he would leave her.

So, pulling on a smile, she lied, "I promise."

* * *

The next morning, Minnie awoke to the beautiful chatter of birds sitting in a tree close to the window. She smiled as she recalled her previous night with Alex. On remembering this, she cocked her face to the side of the bed, but her smile vanished upon seeing it empty.

He was not beside her.

Minnie immediately jumped off the bed and threw his shirt on before grabbing her shorts and dashing out of the room in search of him.

"Alex?" she called out as she walked down the hall to the living room.

Then, she heard some movements in the kitchen, and she hastened towards the source of the sound and entered the kitchen.

Her chest lightened up in flames, and she was sure her stomach did a triple flip at the sight before her. Alex was clad in his tight morning shorts, with his chest bare, and he appeared super sexy. As a plus to this, he had a yellow apron around his waist as he danced his way through his cooking, making the sight adorable.

"Oh!" Minnie laughed.

His eyes flew to the doorway where she stood, and he exclaimed, "Crap!"

This made Minnie laugh even harder. "What's with that look?"

Alex pursed his lips. "You, my dear, have just ruined my idea of breakfast in bed."

"Oh. That's cute." Minnie's eyes widened, but she smiled as she walked to him and wrapped her arms around his torso. "Good morning, Mr. Canaan."

He placed a kiss on her forehead. "You look well refreshed, Ms. Dominique."

Minnie eyed his bare chest, and she bit her lip. "And you look hot in that apron. Super cute but yet seductive," she complimented.

His eyes fell on her lips before trailing back to her eyes, and he laughed once.

"Alright, in that case, BIB would become a daily thing," he said.

Minnie's brows curved up as she chuckled. "What's a BIB?"

Alex laughed again. "Well, my naïve girl, BIB is Breakfast In Bed."

"Smart," Minnie said. "You've got a whole tower of vocabulary up in your head."

He laughed. "Yeah, and there are more cute acronyms from where that came from."

At that moment, she felt light and carefree as satisfaction filled her chest. She stretched herself to her toes and placed a soft kiss on his lips, earning a slight hum from Alex, glad that she had him with her. However, a deliberate cough came from the doorway, making the duo disband from their intimate moment, only to see Nana standing there.

"I hope what's cooking isn't burnt yet?"

Alex and Minnie shared a laugh, but Nana only ogled her eyes at them as she walked into the kitchen, holding her teacup.

"Do you both mind? I wish to eat rather healthy meals from my favorite grandson," Nana added before they all erupted into laughter.

* * *

The rest of the day went faster than Minnie had thought, but this was understandable as she was enjoying her moments with Alex. She didn't bother bringing up the incident with his parents, and Alex seemed to have placed that at the back of his head.

That afternoon, Alex drove to the nearest market, at Nana's request, to get some food supplies, and Minnie tagged along, as she couldn't stay to listen to Nana's boring stories. Nana wasn't unbearable. She was a pleasant woman to be with. However, her stories were long and, most of the time, unimportant to the listener. The reality was Minnie couldn't pass a second to be with Alex, her boyfriend.

The new terminology of her relationship with Alex made her smile all day. This was her first time experiencing love, and for someone who had never thought she'd get to feel loved, this was quite a lot.

"Hey, earth to Minnie." Alex snapped his fingers in front of her face, enough to pull Minnie out of her thoughts, and she faced him absentmindedly. "What's on your mind, gorgeous?"

Minnie beamed. "Nothing."

Alex scoffed. "You're such a terrible liar, Dominique. Speak the truth now, darling," he said.

She laughed. "You know me so well, Alex. However, even though I can, I won't."

He gazed at her, still holding the wheels straight, with a puzzled look in his eyes. "You won't?"

"Yes," Minnie stated.

Alex laughed and faced the road. "At this, you're still a terrible liar."

Minnie chuckled, ignoring him as the car neared the house. She narrowed her eyes as she noticed the three alien vehicles parked at the entrance to the Ardor House. She then felt the car slow down, and on glancing at Alex, she realized he had also noticed the strange cars.

"Expecting visitors?" Minnie asked.

He only mumbled some words too quietly for Minnie to make sense of, but she could tell that the owners of the rides weren't appealing to him.

Alex brought the car to a halt, and he got out, headed to the boot, and Minnie followed. After picking up the bags, Alex approached the house while she just trailed after him. This sucked, as she did not know what was happening, and he did. She felt that he was aware of the visitors, but somehow, he allowed her to remain in the dark.

Minnie cursed under her breath, and she stood in her tracks. Alex also stopped and turned to her, his eyes narrowing at her.

"Why did you stop?" he asked.

The corners of her lips fell downwards, and she crossed her arms in front of her chest and clenched her jaw in determination. "Oh, babe, I am not taking one more step until you tell me what's going on."

His eyebrows became elevated as he watched her for a while before releasing a pronounced sigh. "C'mon, Minnie, not now, please."

Minnie had her mind made. She wasn't heading in until he let her into his thoughts. To make her point, she curled her lips up, crouched to the ground, and squatted.

"Seriously, Minnie?"

Frowning, she stated, "I wasn't kidding."

Instead of speaking, Alex walked to her with a huge smile, dropped the bags, and pulled her up effortlessly until he brought her to stand on her feet, and she pouted at him.

"It's not fair!" she said. "Why do you have to be so strong?"

He chuckled. "To be able to pull your hilarious self from your moods. I think it's pretty fair."

Minnie rolled her eyes inwardly at him. "Whatever."

"You are a crazy girl, Dominique."

Minnie smirked, raised her shoulders, and threw her arms around his waist. "I admit. However, you are an un-crazy gofer."

Alex laughed harder. "Right on point."

"So," Minnie began, her eyes glancing toward the unfamiliar cars, and she asked, "Who are the visitors?"

As soon as the words left her lips, Alex's laugh faded into the mist as he followed her gaze, glancing at the house, watching for a while, before saying in a small voice, "Probably my uncle and my twin."

Minnie raised a brow, wondering why they would be there. She soon face-palmed herself when she recalled Nana was their relation too.

"Your uncle?" she finally asked.

He nodded. "Yes, my uncle, Dad's brother, Madison's father."

"Oh," Minnie said. "Your twin, too?"

"Yes, his only copy."

She heard a bolder voice reply to her, and both she and Alex spun around to the owner. Standing before them was Alex's replica, and for a second, Minnie felt her eyes whip in shock at the resemblance between the twins. A replica was an understatement to describe the man standing before them. He was Alex in a different mode of dressing, hairstyle, and outlook.

Minnie turned her gaze to Alex.

As if reading her mind, he smiled faintly before speaking. "Dominique, meet my twin brother—" he started but couldn't complete the introductions as his brother cut in with a broad grin, a hand stretched for a shake and a sly look in his eyes.

"I'm Andrew J. Canaan, his twin brother."

* * *

Minutes passed in a flash. Minnie kept her gaze on Alexander's twin, Andrew. He looked like her boyfriend, and it was almost impossible to tell them apart. Andrew was equally buffed as his slicked muscles spoke of his frequent gym visits, just like Alex's. His face was shaved, save for a slight brush on the rim of his lips. His eyes had the same crystallized sparkle as that of his brother, but his stare seemed quite daunting and intimidating.

Minnie noticed Andrew had a bold tattoo on the back of his right ear. It was an inscription of some sort, but she couldn't make meaning of the words. The only similarity the brothers shared, apart from their physical cloning, was that both seemed to take an interest in being living art portraits. The brothers were tattoo freaks. Andrew barely had any skin uninked.

A warm hand cupped hers, pulling her out of her thoughts, and she turned to meet Alexander's soft gaze while Andrew dropped his hand after realizing that Minnie wasn't interested in accepting his handshake.

"Oh, you've grown so much since I last saw you, Alex."

The trio turned to the front of the house, where a much older-looking man stood, slightly resembling Alex's father. He was stout, and despite the wrinkles at the side of his eyes, he still looked fresh.

Behind him were Nana and Madison. Minnie's eyes remained on the strange man in their midst. She strained her eyes to inspect him as he was very familiar to her, and she couldn't push away the strong thought that she had a very close relationship with him.

"Vincent!"

Alex called from behind her. Her jaw flung open, and her eyes went wide in recognition. Her heart skipped a beat, and bile rushed from beneath her stomach to her mouth, but she forcefully gulped it down as she kept staring at the man in shock.

Vincent's lips crawled down at the edges, and he folded his arms in front of his chest.

"I know you don't fancy my presence here, nephew, but could you not be this unaccommodating to me?" he asked.

Beside her, Alex scoffed. "No."

Andrew flipped into a laugh at his brother's statement, and Minnie could barely hold back her shock on seeing Vincent, after all these years, after what had happened between them. Even if she tried to shove all these down the drain of her mind, the images of what had transpired between them flashed before her eyes.

Vincent's eyes darted over to her and met her eyes for a second, but Minnie forcefully tore her gaze from him, finally regaining consciousness of herself. However, she did not miss the smile that curved up the side of his brown lips on seeing her, and at once, she knew she was done for.

He recalled her. He remembered everything.

A slight squeeze on her palm caused her to turn to face her side, and she looked up to meet Alex's eyes. His brows were raised in worry. He cocked his head to her and, in a small whisper, asked, "Are you alright?"

Even though her mind was clouded and her tongue caught up in her throat, she managed a nod and forced a small smile.

His lips shifted up in response to this, but she knew better. He was still worried.

If he knew the truth, then maybe the look he'd have would be more of scorn and hatred at who she truly was, who she had kept away from him.

Could she not have to deal with her bad luck now? Why was the universe always allowing her past to shadow her?"

A deliberate cough came from behind her, and Minnie and Alex turned to Andrew, who had a playful smile etched on his face.

"Brother, you haven't introduced your lady friend to us yet," he said.

This only made matters worse as everyone looked at Minnie, and her feet became cold in her sandals. She moved closer to Alex, interlacing her fingers with his in an attempt to hide from their eyes.

Alex reacted to this by firming their grip. He ignored his brother and leaned towards her. He dropped his voice to a whisper and said, "Minnie, "Let's go in."

Minnie agreed, and both walked in after grabbing their shopping, sparing no one another look.

* * *

Several questions throbbed the walls of her mind as she sat on the bed, her head on Alex's shoulders and her mind replaying the events of her past with Vincent. Alex had not uttered a word since they walked out on his uncle, brother, Nana, and Madison. He also seemed clouded in the maze of his thoughts as he kept staring into space, almost as if he wasn't there beside her. She didn't have the mind to worry about him, as she was also drawn into the depths of her thoughts.

When she had thought she had finally escaped the clutches of her clogged past, the delirious fate brought back a nefarious figure from her past to haunt her.

This was her doom. This was what she had feared.

How could she escape Vincent speaking about what had transpired between the two of them years ago?

Indeed, Vincent was one of the recurrent and eminent clients of the brothel. He was one of her customers, one with a webbed connection with the girl she used to be, who Dinah had created.

Vincent had been one of the many men from the elite world who had requested her personally. So, there was no way he would miss her face, even in a crowd, or forget her. She knew this day would arrive, but she had not expected it would be this soon, in the extant condition and with Alex involved.

No, she could not lose him.

If he found out about her past, she'd be done with. He would ditch her, and she will revert to her old miserable self. She would become a loner, with no one to care for or to be cared for. She would have no one to love and to love her in return.

No, she could not go back to that.

Minnie had to stop these events before the worst happened, but she did not know what to do. Her mind was jumbled up in her head as everything was so messed up, but she couldn't give up, not yet, at least.

Even in her dilemma, Minnie couldn't help but worry about Alex. She was at a crossroads with her demons, but Alex was all that truly mattered to her. After all, he was still hers, and she was still his.

He seemed to be buried under the weight of his troubles. Minnie needed to know why, but she did not want to weigh him by forcing him to speak up.

The least she could do was to be there for him as he would for her. After all, this is all she ever wanted to be.

Couldn't it be just her and him? Couldn't the world leave them be? Couldn't everything be perfect without all these trials and obstacles impeding their love?

She took a deep breath to pull herself together, and she stroked his hand wrapped around her waist as she relaxed into his chest. The feeling of his chest rising and falling made her warm and gave her confirmation that he was there with her.

This was unusual. His attitude was off. It felt as though Alexander was caging himself into a box, and she couldn't get to him.

Firming her jaws, she drew him back to reality, back to her.

She cocked her chin to his face and caught him staring at her. As soon as their eyes met, he let out a small smile, but this was just a slight shift at the edge of his lips. She could sense the sadness within him, and she wanted nothing but to overshadow that.

Minnie only wished she could soar on the wings of perfection with him – if only wishes came true. As illusionary as that might seem, she could do her best and try, right?

She pulled herself up to her knees beside him on the bed. His eyes followed her as she threw herself over his legs until she was practically sitting on his lap, and then she placed her arms around his neck, locking her gaze with him instantly.

"Alex, what's with the long face?" she questioned, but he sighed and held her waist, pulling her close to himself without saying a word.

Minnie felt her heart drop, but she kept a straight face. This was hard – getting Alex to ease up whenever he was tensed. She had done this before, so she could do it again.

She leaned into him and placed her lips on his, kissing him with all unspoken emotions, with all affection, with all desire, and with all her love.

Alexander did not hold back as he returned the intensity of her kiss.

This was perfect. If only they could remain like this forever, everything would be A-Okay. They would be alright as long as it was her and him together, eternally.

Minnie could feel the warmth of his body, his comfortable grip around her, reminding her of the safety she had felt whenever she was with him. She also felt the uncertainties that ran through his mind, his pain, and felt his disappointment. She could understand all the emotions raging in his mind.

Drawing out of their kiss, Alex ran his tongue over his lower lip, probably longing for more than just a kiss. His eyes lifted to meet hers, his hands leaving her waist, trailing slowly down her lap.

"Minnie, I am fine, trust me," he said.

Minnie knew better. He was lying. He was trying to be strong, trying to act as if all was okay. He was feigning it. They both pretended that all was up to scratch.

She shook her head. "No, you're not."

"Minnie, I am with you around," he said and pulled her closer to himself, his hands trailing to the inner of her thigh, circling at places he knew was sensitive to her, and he was right as slight moans escaped from her lips.

Alexander brought his face to her neck, burying it at the side of her face.

Speaking into her ear in a slight whisper, he said, "I love you, Dominique, and you'll understand these soonest. I'll not keep a thing from you, I promise."

Minnie smiled dryly. If only she could do the same — if only she could be honest and come clean to him.

"It's alright," she breathed.

Gratified, he kissed the lobe of her ear, tracing kisses down her neck and proceeding to her chest as his hands worked her legs, causing his breath to become hotter and his touches more sensitive on her skin.

Then, snapping them both out of their fantasies, the door flew open with a loud creak, and a grumble from Alex followed this as he let out a disappointed sigh.

Minnie climbed down from him, and they threw their eyes at the smirking idiot in the doorway.

"I did not know you were busy. Vincent wishes to see you, bro," Andrew said as his eyes danced between Minnie and Alex.

Andrew's eyes lingered on Minnie, burning through her skin, causing her skin to tingle. This was too much for her comfort.

Alex probably noticed the lustful glances his brother was throwing toward Minnie as his lips curled into a sneer, and he snapped, "Message delivered. You can leave now, Andrew."

Disappointed, Andrew bit his lower lip before tearing his eyes away from Minnie and retracting out of the room, leaving the couple.

Alex tugged on her hand, and she faced him.

"Let's go meet them and hear what they've got to say."

"So, you're okay now?" Minnie asked.

A genuine smile crossed his lips, and he said, "With you, I always am."

"Okeydokey, let's move, Mr. Canaan," she joked, pulling his arm with her as she stood up, and he followed her with a laugh.

"As her majesty pleases." He chuckled.

As soon as he was firmly on his feet, she moved into his arms and wrapped her arms around his body, enveloping him in a warm embrace.

"Hey, babe, it's all right," he cooed as he stroked her back.

Minnie looked up at his face, pursing her lips as she pouted, saying, "Promise me you wouldn't try this again."

His smile dimpled his cheeks, and he kissed the top of her head and said, "Promise."

With this, they walked out of the room to meet Alex's kin. Even though Minnie wasn't ready to deal with Vincent, she had to support Alex and hoped that Vincent would never recall who she was and what transpired between them three years ago.

Though it seemed impossible, she could only hope.

* * *

They returned to the main room where Alex's uncle, twin brother, and Nana were seated, engrossed in whatever they had cordially chosen as a topic of interest, but as soon as the couple stepped into the room, they stopped and faced them.

"You've come out, finally, Alex," Vincent announced.

This earned him a scoff from Alex, who stood beside Minnie, his face twisted into a frown, and his hand held securely in hers.

Minnie was not a mind reader, but she could decipher that Alex and Vincent weren't exactly on good terms. Alex appeared to desire the company of anyone else but his uncle. She did not know what the backstory was, but it was apparent his relationship with his uncle was sour.

"Why are you here?" Alex asked.

Vincent's brows curved at this, though Minnie could tell he was not surprised at his nephew's question.

"C'mon, Alexander, can't an old uncle visit his favorite nephews anymore?" he asked, and then glanced at Madison with a smile before adding, "Besides, I missed my little girl."

Madison shoved her face to the side, avoiding Vincent's eyes, and Minnie's expression closed up as she noticed Madison's reaction. Could it be that Vincent also had a distant relationship with his daughter, as with Alex?

She had no more time to think about this as Alex spoke up, replying to Vincent. "You have no relation here, Vincent," he said. "No one here really wants you around."

Vincent laughed. His laughter appeared to be a sad chortle to cover how deeply hurt he was at Alexander's words. Despite what experience she had with him, Minnie believed that this was too much, even for him.

However, Vincent swallowed this – obviously without a choice – and stood from the couch and walked towards the couple, stopping only a few feet from them.

His eyes were initially on Alex, but on nearing them, his gaze shifted to Minnie, and his eyes narrowed on her.

Minnie froze as she felt the bile rise from the bottom of her throat to her mouth. The way his eyes stared at her caused the recollection of what she had with him to return.

His lips shifted into a small smirk as his eyes lit up in recognition. Minnie was more than assured he recalled who she was and every single memory.

"You look very familiar, young lady. Do I know you?" he asked.

What Vincent failed to recall was that his nephew was still present, and even though he had to have noticed how pale Minnie was and suspected that she must have something to do with him, Alexander gave her palm a slight squeeze.

He had given her his word. He would remain supportive and wait till she was ready to share her story with him.

Minnie's troubled mind calmed as soon as she felt his warmth over her palm, and she knew she wasn't alone. He was there for her.

Vincent had no opportunity to continue his questions towards Minnie as his nephew's attention was drawn to his acts.

"Why are you here, Vincent?" Alex asked again.

Vincent pulled his face into a straight smile, trying to look as honest and serious as he could, and answered, "I'm simply here to spend some time with my mother, your grandmother, and my little girl."

Alex scoffed. "That isn't the truth," he stated.

Vincent's smile fell instantly, and he sniggered but didn't give a reply to Alex. His eyes wandered back to Minnie, and an acidic bile flipped through her, moving to the base of her tongue.

She felt his eyes burn through her, and she could feel the uneasy sensation in her belly grow worse. She was disgusted at the man's sight and the stubborn unpleasant memories that refused to leave her head.

How she wished God would save her from her situation, but she laughed to herself. Why would God help her? Of all creatures he made, why would he choose to save her? She was nothing but filth who had not only menaced the man in front of her, but she had also done more unimaginable things with him for money. She was a sinner, and again, she queried her actions: was she supposed to be here in the first place? Did she easily forget who she was? Oh, how funny she thought loving Alex would solely wash away her past depravities and give her a new identity.

No, her past was going to catch up with her, and Vincent was here to start that.

"I believe I asked a question, Vincent," Alex restated.

From behind them came Andrew's voice, saying, "He's here because I gave him permission."

Alex's brows snapped together as he spun around to his brother. Andrew was standing at the doorway, his back leaning comfortably on the wall, his eyes dazzling with smugness, and his lips carrying a full smirk.

It was unbelievable that Andrew had shared a womb with Alex as he was so different and full of himself – a jerk at the greatest level.

"Who gave you that right?" Alex said through gritted teeth.

Andrew laughed. "Being your brother gave me that right. Man, this is grandma's house. We are all entitled to be here. Vincent is grandmother's son, and he is also your uncle."

Unruffled by this, Alex maintained. "This house belonged to Dominion Canaan, our grandfather, who bestowed this house to me as an inheritance, and in all legal terms, I am the owner and determinant of all that goes on in, around, and with this house."

Minnie gaped at how Alex composed himself and how assertively he spoke to his brother.

Exhaustedly, Andrew threw his hands up. "You are hopeless, Alex," he said and glanced at Vincent, saying. "I tried, but this is pointless."

With this, Andrew walked to an empty sofa and crashed into it.

Vincent's lips parted as though he wanted to object to this, but he soon calmed himself and, with a gentle smile, said, "I mean no trouble, Alexander. I only have business here, and so, I thought, why not spend the time with my family?"

Alex laughed. "Yeah, I believe it is too late for that," he said, then paused as he eyed Vincent before continuing, "When are you leaving?"

Vincent drew a long breath before answering, "Soon."

Alex frowned. "How soon?"

"Just two weeks," Vincent said.

"Alright. You have two weeks. Then, you get out, understood?" Alex stated.

For a while, Minnie had to remind herself that he was speaking to his uncle, not just an employee or a random person. However, she understood that Alex couldn't simply hate Vincent. He must have done the worst to warrant the coldness from Alex, and she only wondered what he had done.

Nana stood to her feet and walked to Alex. In a small voice, she said, "Jose, despite all he's done, you do not have to speak to him in that manner. He's always going to be your uncle, come what may."

Defeated, Alex sighed. "It's alright, Nana. As long as he stays in his lane, I'll stay on mine."

"I trust your words, my boy." Nana smiled.

Alex turned to Minnie, and at once, she knew he was signaling her to go with him, and they both walked out of the house and into the car.

He unlocked and got in, but Minnie remained at the gate watching him. He despised Vincent, and she was curious to know the reason, even though she knew she would soon have her share of the troubles. However, she was selfishly glad that they weren't on good terms because if not, she would have been exposed. She couldn't be that heartless. She wished the best for Alex, as he was all she cared about. He had confided and trusted in her, but she had kept mountains of secrets from him when he deserved to know the whole truth about her identity.

"Minnie?"

She jumped at hearing his call and realized that he had driven the car to her front, waiting for her to get in.

She stood straight and got into the vehicle beside him. After tucking herself in, Alex drove out of the premises.

"Babe?"

With his gaze on the front, he answered, "Um?"

She traced her hand on his, resting on the console between them, and she interlocked their fingers.

"It's going to be okay," she reassured.

He glanced at her, a small smile resting on the base of his lips. "I know because I have you."

Minnie smiled, but this was a farce to how she felt. How could she be there for him when she held back so much from him?

Alex brought her hand to his lips and grazed her knuckles with his lower lip. "I trust you, Minnie, because I love you more than life itself."

Minnie blanched, and she did not notice that Alex stopped the car and parked it on the side of the road.

He turned to her and pulled her hands to himself before placing a kiss on her palms.

"Minnie, please do not keep a thing from me," he said.

Locking his eyes with hers, Alex asked, "Is there anything you want to tell me, Dominique? Anything at all? I am ready to listen to you."

This was it! He wanted to know all about her. He was asking that she confide in him. However, could she trust him?

Seven

Alex drove around the area for a while, but there was dead silence in the car, as Minnie was lost in the sphere of her thoughts, while Alex was also unusually quiet. Something was off with his quietness, and Minnie couldn't help but fear that he was drifting away from her, and maybe, he had already figured her out. His hands were on the wheel as he drove past a familiar tree, and it occurred to her that he was driving in circles, probably to burn off his thoughts.

She was to blame for his dilemma, as the guilt of not telling him the truth kept eating through her. She loved him but knew it would break him if he learned of her past. He'd feel betrayed. He'd hate her, and he may cease to trust again.

"Minnie?"

She turned to him. "Yes?"

"Are you alright?"

"I-I am fine." She stuttered. "Are you?"

He nodded. "I am."

"Are you sure, Alexander?" She persisted.

He smiled and faced the road. For a moment, he stared ahead, and the silence returned. Minnie nervously latched her fingers, hoping he would speak to her. She needed to know what he was thinking. She had to see if she had messed up.

Why could she not confide in the man she loved? Couldn't the threads of the past be weaved away? *Why is it that the joy of her future is buried under the rocks of lies, and the melody of her heart stung with the twigs of denial?*

"Fire."

His voice returned, and she brightened.

"Oak and the guys are waiting for us."

She raised a brow. "They are?"

He nodded. "There's a race coming up, and…"

"You want to participate?" she chimed in.

His lips stretched into a smile. "Yes, love, and I want you to be my…"

Minnie did not wait for him to complete this as she shook her head.

"No."

He chuckled. "But I haven't even asked."

"My answer is no, Alexander. I'm not going to be in that car with you," she insisted, recalling her experience with their race.

"Minnie," he cooed. "Just this once."

She caught the sparkle in his eyes as they rounded into a puppy plea, which was sincere. He was happy, and she wanted him to always be happy. So, she could endure whatsoever, just for him.

"Fine."

His eyes lit up, but she held her finger and added, "Just this once because you begged."

His smile deepened as he reached for her hand and gave it a light squeeze.

"Thanks."

Satisfied, Minnie relaxed into the seat, grateful to have evaded losing him.

* * *

On returning to the house, Minnie retreated into the room, locking herself in after Alex left to meet with his friends. She was left at home with Nana, Andrew, and Vincent. Judging by how Vincent kept staring at her, she knew he recalled everything, which sent chills down her spine. No matter how long she kept the truth from getting exposed, she would eventually have to come clean.

Although Alex had promised to return in an hour, she was terrified at the thought of Vincent coming around her. Yet, she could not share this with him due to her lies. Rather, she lay in her bed with her arms wrapped around the pillow, which made her calm and reminded her of his presence.

A slight knock on the door snapped through the serenity she had created in her mind, and through the side of her eye, she stared at the door. She watched it for a while, but when she heard nothing, she closed her eyes, humming to herself, but the knock came again, this time louder, and Minnie sat up.

This could not be Alex, so she wondered who it might be.

Pulling herself together, she asked, "Who's there?"

All she received was nothing.

She stood from the bed and walked to the door.

"Alex?" she called in a small voice, but no one answered.

She reached for the doorknob, unlocked it, and opened the door, only to wish she hadn't, as the person behind the door was none other than the person she did not want to see. With his body leaning in the doorway, his hands in his pocket, and a rueful smirk on his face, Vincent, apparently loved her current expression.

"Sweet Minnie, it's a pleasure to meet you again," he said

Minnie froze, her lips glued together.

He laughed. "Why do you look so surprised?"

Struggling to get herself back, she stuttered, "Why are you here?"

His smirk widened, and his eyes grew dark as he moved to her. "And, I thought you had no remembrance of me."

"What are you doing here, Vincent?" She gritted.

Without replying, he placed his palm on the door and pushed it open. Before Minnie could stop him, he found his way into the room, shoving her aside.

"Get out!" she yelled.

But he crossed his arms and eyed her. As his eyes danced over her, her mind wandered off to recollecting what had transpired between them years ago.

* * *

Chatters of young girls echoed down the halls of the brothel's main room, where about twenty young girls sat, each with a book or a newspaper that Dinah had kept for them. After all, she needed the girls to be, to some extent, literate and thus encouraged reading.

Through the slightly opened windows, light rays flashed into the room, and their cheerful chatters died as they looked at the light rays.

One of the girls stood and glanced through the window to see that three big cars had driven into the premises. "The men are here!" she announced.

Just like that, the girls rose from their positions, knowing well that their miseries were about to begin, and they all filed out of the room, dispersing to get prepared. These men were big special patrons of the brothel who were favorites of Dinah, as each visit left her with big stacks of cash.

Several of these men were politicians, businessmen, generals, billionaires, and dealers of all sorts, so they were quite powerful, and whenever they were around, no other customer had access to the brothel. They owned the night, as they got to choose what, whose, and how they wanted their service.

The parade began as soon as the girls got dressed in their special seductive outfits and lined in the center of the premises. The parade was solely for these men to select their choice.

Being the star at the brothel, Minnie was attired and prepared by Dinah herself, as she had faith that the men would always ask for the best, and this was Minnie. She was in a pink mini skirt, under which she had a pair of white thongs, and above, she wore a white tank top that stopped above her abdomen. This was perfect for Dinah as Minnie was ready.

The others were first walked in front of the men before she was brought out, and the spotlight fell on her as all the men turned their attention towards her.

One of the men, a fat, short, black man attired in the famous 'agbada,' raised his hand. "I will pay double for her."

Before Dinah could react to this, another said, "Triple."

This turned into a bet, as each man placed their amounts down. However, the one who sat farthest from them cleared his throat and said in his deep voice, "Name your price."

"I'll pay anything and everything to have her," he added, much to the shock of everyone in the room, including Minnie.

Dinah didn't need to stress the night further, as Minnie knew who had won her for the night. Of course, the man was none other than Vincent Canaan, who was called VC.

That night, he made her do things she never could forget. He did horrific things to her body, explored her beyond places he should have, and she was sure he enjoyed every bit of it. That night everything changed about her. At that moment, she felt utterly used and despoiled, which only aggravated her hatred towards men.

She cursed that day and prayed she would never have a cause to recall it, but there she was, standing a few meters from the same man who had used her years ago.

* * *

"I'm honored you remember us, Dominique," Vincent said.

Minnie looked up through her tears that almost clouded her sight as the hurt and pain she had tried to bury away resurfaced. She pursed her lips and stared at him with despise.

"Get out now, Vincent!" she spat.

He wasn't prepared to listen. He moved to her and grabbed her arm.

She tried to yank her arm back, but his grip was too tight; his fingers dug into her skin, and she groaned in pain.

"Let me go!" she cried.

He laughed. "I own you, sweet Minnie, you and the whole of you," he pointed out to her.

"You don't!" she snapped at him

Vincent laughed even harder and pushed her down. Before she could get up, he was already on her and pinned her to the mattress with his strong arms.

"Please, Vincent, get off me," she begged and tried to push his body off her, but it was of no use as he pressed her into the mattress and cocked his head to her neck, placing his cold lips on her skin.

She flinched as she did not want him to have his way with her, not again. Desperately, she snapped her head to his arm, dug her teeth into his skin, and bit him as hard as she could. Shrieking in pain, he released her, and she jumped away from him, but he gripped her and pulled her back to him.

"Damn you, bitch!"

Before she could stop him, he slapped her across her face.

Minnie fell to the bed as her face was twisted to the side by his hit, and she cried out.

* * *

Throbs erupted from the side of her face, feeling tears threatening to break from her eyes, yet she knew crying was pointless. Vincent was stronger than her, but she could not let him overpower her.

Without thinking, she raised her knee and kicked Vincent in the groin. His face contorted in pain before he rolled off her, clutching his hurt self.

Minnie immediately jumped off the bed but was shocked when she saw Andrew in the doorway, his gaze fixated on them. His eyes were blank and unreadable as he stared at them.

Finally, his lips parted, and he spoke. "What just happened?"

Minnie was at a loss for words, and she just stared at him helplessly.

Vincent wasn't mute. He said, in a little cracked voice, "Nothing."

"Nothing?" Andrew asked, raising a brow. "You mean all this is nothing, Vincent?"

Shocked at his nephew's response, Vincent drooped, and in a pleading tone, he begged, "I can explain."

Andrew laughed. "Yeah, sure. Go ahead and explain, Vincent. Explain to me how you were about to force your nephew's girlfriend."

A wave of relief washed over Minnie when she heard his words. He understood what was about to happen and saved her from explaining. Yet, she could not tell if he was taking her side.

Vincent was stumped. "Andrew, that wasn't what happened." He tried to reason with his nephew, but Andrew was adamant – something he shared in common with his twin brother.

Adding to ignoring Vincent, Andrew turned to her and asked, "Are you alright?"

Minnie nodded. "I am."

Despite her joy at Andrew's attitude, Minnie was skeptical about his true intentions. Was he going to use this as a sort of blackmail? Would he inform his brother? If he did, then all her secrets would be revealed, as Alex would be prompted to find out what had led Vincent to the room.

After walking out of the room, Minnie stepped into the open air, allowing the freshness to fill her.

Andrew had followed, leaving Vincent speechless and stomped. Vincent had attempted to plead his way with his nephew, but Andrew was not ready to listen to whatever he had to say.

"Please, Andrew."

Angered, Andrew frowned. "Why are you even still speaking?"

"I—" Vincent stammered.

"Just cut it," Andrew cut him off. "I am disappointed in you."

With this, both he and Minnie walked out of the room.

Following the incident, Minnie sat on the grass in the backyard of the Ardor house. She was perturbed by the events that had led her to that moment. She had been so close to getting screwed by her boyfriend's uncle, and he would have succeeded as he knew she could not muster the courage to confess such to Alex. This was true as if she had the guts, she should have spilled all her heart's content to Alex, but she had soared on with the lies and deceit that were fixated in her mind and reflected in her actions.

Staring into the distance, Minnie wandered deep into her thoughts. The air was still, but the sky was grey, and everywhere was quiet. The weather was gloomy, just like her emotions, clouded and unstable.

She was a selfish individual.

Alexander did not deserve this. He should not be kept in darkness when he was a source of light in her life. He had not held anything from her, yet, all about her remained a sealed confidential file to him. He had never brought up the question of her past again. He believed that they should focus on the future, but she was being unfair with her lies.

Minnie sighed. She had to tell him, and she had to be fast about it.

Vincent was not going to give up on ripping every bit of her, and well, she could not tell what Andrew would do on his part. His interference in her life meant she was now treading on a thin line.

"Dominique."

She was pulled out of her thoughts and turned to meet Andrew's calm posture.

"Hey, it's alright. It's I."

Minnie nodded with a slight smile. She was still shaken, and she could not tell if it was because she had escaped Vincent's antics or the fact that Andrew had saved her or that sooner or later, Alex was going to walk in, and his brother would tell him everything.

Andrew draped his arms around her shoulder, and she shook.

"You need to calm down."

"I'm fine." She forged a broader smile.

To this, he smiled, and for the first time, his appearance reminded her of Alex, as he looked so innocent and good.

"I know you're pretending, but I'll leave you be," he said as he sat beside her.

Minnie tensed up again.

"Calm down, Minnie. I only want to help."

"I don't need your help."

Minnie did not know what tripped her, but she wanted to be alone, away from everyone except Alex. Her actions must have perplexed Andrew as he shifted farther from her, and all that remained was silence. She was hard on him, but she was too full of troubles. She was wrecked. If not, why would she yell at someone who had helped her?

Andrew stared ahead, and she bit her lower lip in regret.

"I'm sorry," she mumbled.

He smiled. "I understand, Minnie," he said, "I can call you Minnie, right?"

"Sure."

He nodded and looked back at the front. Another couple of silent minutes passed before Minnie broke it with a small cough.

"Um, thanks for saving my ass back there."

He eyed her. "Why thank me? Girl, you handled it well."

"Uh?"

He chuckled. "Vincent was, well, he was down before I could react. You are one strong and brave lady, and you can sure take care of yourself."

"Thanks." She smiled.

"By the way, what happened in there?" he asked.

"Uh, what do you mean?"

Andrew stared hard at her before replying. "I'm not justifying his actions, but I know Vincent, and he's not one to jump at girls that way. What's special in your case?"

His words struck her, and she became mute.

Continuing, he said, "It feels like there's some connection between you both. Is this right?"

She blinked and forced herself together.

"No, you are not right," she said.

"Oh! That's okay."

She raised a brow at him. "Ok?"

Andrew laughed and draped his arm around her shoulder. "It's alright. I want to be sure that you are okay, and Vincent's only the promiscuous bloke he has always been."

Minnie forced an uncomfortable smile, and she scooted away from him. Luckily, Andrew understood her as he withdrew his hand. However, Minnie still needed assurance of Andrew's concealment. She was certain Vincent would not have the guts to tell his nephew of his actions, but she was not sure about the man beside her. She had to make sure he never told his brother.

"Andrew, can you do me a favor?"

"A favor?"

Minnie nodded. "Can you keep this a secret?"

"A secret?"

"Yes, please," she begged, her pulse roaring in her throat as she crossed her fingers.

Andrew kept his eyes locked with hers without replying.

She wondered anxiously. *Would he help me, or would he proceed to ruin me?*

Rustling sounds from behind them broke their gaze.

"Minnie?"

On hearing Alex's voice, her heart stumbled over its rhythm, and at once, she turned to him.

Wrinkles spread across his forehead at her reaction, but this soon miraged into worry.

"Are you alright, Fire?"

She stared at him, wanting desperately to reply, but her lips quivered at the thought of forming another lie, yet, her throat went bitter at the attempt at the truth. She wanted to come clean to him, but another part of her kept replaying scenarios of what the outcome of her truth might be.

Seeing she was quiet, Alex shifted his gaze to his brother, who had also stood up.

"What happened?"

Once again, Minnie's heart thundered, scared that Andrew would go ahead and speak, but she still hoped he would not.

Andrew's eyes wandered to hers, and they held the gaze for a second before he returned to his brother. "Nothing happened, bro," he lied. "I was keeping your girlfriend's company since she was so worried about you," he added.

Alex turned to her, and a gentle smile ripped through his lips. Convinced, he said, "Thanks, I guess."

"No problem, bro." Andrew smiled. "I should take my leave now that you are back," he added and returned to the house.

Minnie could not contain her happiness that he did not snitch on her.

"Minnie?"

"Hey."

He moved to her, his brows knitted with worry and his hands hesitant. "What is wrong, Fire?"

The rapid pounding of her heart reminded her that she had to tell him the truth. Despite getting away from Andrew telling on her, she could not bear the thought of another slip-up. She could not keep lying to the man she loved.

Alex's worry heightened, and he reached for her hands, clasping them with his. "C'mon, Minnie, what the devil is going on with you?"

Her eyes moistened as she realized she did not dare to tell him. She could not watch him hate her. She could not lose him. She couldn't accept that after telling him, he would be gone.

She stared into his orbs, wishing he could see her hesitations; she wanted him to read her feelings without her words.

Reluctantly, she pealed her lips apart and began, "Alex, I—"

Vincent suddenly appeared and jumped into their conversation. His eyes were red, and his expression was bland.

"I can see you are back, Alexander," Vincent said.

"Of course, I'm back," Alex replied. "What's with the absurd statement?"

Vincent laughed. "Oh. I don't know who is truly absurd: I or you?" he stated.

Through the corner of her eye, Minnie noticed the wicked glint he had on, and she slumped, knowing he was going to expose her.

Alex quizzed, "What do you mean?"

The glint in Vincent's eyes sparkled, and his lips curled into a smirk. "Have you cared to know who you are associating with?"

"Cut the chase, Vincent," Alex scorned.

Vincent laughed again. "Those you trust, how well do you know them?"

His eyes flashed towards Minnie. It was definite he had planned his words, and everything he would say would revolve around her, no one but her.

"I don't understand—" Alex tried to say.

"What do you know of her?" Vincent cut in.

Minnie was afraid to blink. He had brought her up, and what did she do? She just stood there like a dummy and watched the words roll out of his lips.

"Do you know the woman you claim to trust? Do you know the woman you love? The true her?" Vincent asked.

Alex turned to her, and their gaze met. For a moment, it was as if he was trying to read her expression while she just stared, shocked and speechless. Then, he looked away from her and returned his hard gaze to Vincent.

"Why does this matter to you?" Alex asked.

Vincent was taken aback by this while Minnie frowned.

"Whoever told you that I do not know Dominique?" he asked.

Minnie stared at him, dumbfounded at his reaction, but she wasn't the only one, as Vincent looked like he had been slapped hard.

Unfortunately for Vincent, Alex wasn't done. "You speak of trust, Vincent, but what have you done to earn the trust of those you know? What have you done to those you claim to love?" he questioned.

This struck Vincent even harder, and this was obvious by the way his eyes were wide. Minnie was also as taken aback as he was at Alex's words.

Still, Alex continued, "My dad knew you. He trusted you; we all did, and we loved you, but what did we get in return?" he asked, his eyes stern and his voice fierce. "You betrayed us – you stole from us and even made decisions to our detriment, dashing all our beliefs in knowing you."

Alex took a break and glared at his uncle. "Now, you have the guts to tell me I don't know who I love."

He took two steps toward Vincent and stopped an arm's length from him. Staring him in the eyes, he said, "You know nothing of love and trust. Thus, you have no effing right to question Dominique because she is far more deserving of love and trust than you.

"So, as an answer to your ludicrous question, Vincent, I do know the woman I love, and I trust her because despite what might have happened to her in the past, she did not let it determine who she is and who she would become.

"I do not care who Dominique was before, as all that matters is her present times," he said, and a smile rippled on his face as he threw a glance at Minnie. "I know Dominique; I trust her and will forever love her, come what may."

He had just confessed that he would love her forever. Minnie was ecstatic and wished she could feel like a victor, but she knew the worst was yet to come – she still had to tell Alex the truth.

Alex grasped her palm and led her away from the stumped Vincent, and they walked towards the house.

* * *

"Did you mean what you said?" Minnie asked as Alex held her against the wall of the room.

Instead of replying, he brought his face to hers until there was no space between them. He raised his palm to her face and cupped her cheek.

"Minnie, do you doubt me?"

There was no use in trying to confirm what he said. Even if he repeated it a million times, Minnie would not believe it, as she couldn't count herself worthy of his love. She couldn't when she kept lying to him and herself.

"Alex," she breathed. "I've held too much from you. Why would you stand up for me in Vincent's presence?"

His lips curved into a dimpled smile. He brushed his fingers over her ear and tucked a strand of her hair behind it. "Minnie," he breathed, his eyes on her hair. "I did mean it when I said I'll wait till you're ready to tell me about yourself."

Returning his eyes to hers, he said, "However, I got to know you, I got to understand you, and I got to respect you. It no longer mattered to know your past, as I love who you are and not who you were. I love you and not the circumstances that surrounded you.

"Dominique, we all have our secrets, but that would never stop us from loving each other, would it? I respect your privacy, and I know someday, you will share them with me. I have no idea when that will be, but I will be waiting."

Minnie bit her lower lip, and she closed her eyes as she felt a teardrop slide down her cheek but was stopped by his thumb. She opened her eyes and caught him staring at her. She was tired of holding the lies in her heart. She wanted to be free; she wanted to be normal; she wanted to be worthy of his love.

In Alexander's eyes, she found the reassurance that he was there with her and he would not leave. He was asking her to trust him and release herself unto him.

So, with all the confidence she could muster up, she spilled the truth.

"I was a child-sex worker."

His eyes widened. "What?"

"Alex, I…" She tried to say, but again, her words were reluctant to come forth.

"Dominique, I do not understand what you are trying to say."

Tears filled her eyes, almost clouding her view, as she began. "Alex, if I show you my flaws, would you still love me? If I told you the truth, would you still love me?"

His forehead wrinkled. "Minnie, you are starting to scare me."

She took a deep breath, exhaled it, and said, "I was a prostitute. Not just any. I was a star at it. As a child, I did sex for money. I am totally impure. I've been ravaged and broken, and…"

Unable to continue, she stared into his eyes, but they were frozen. They just stared at each other for several seconds, and then he blinked once and moved back.

"What do you mean?" He stuttered.

"I…"

"C'mon, answer me, Dominique!" he yelled

Minnie trembled.

He had never raised his voice at her, but now, he was so angered at her, and she began to rethink her actions. But it was too late to go back. So, she was determined to tell him everything.

"Alex, I am an orphan, and I was raised by a woman called Dinah. She owned the most prominent brothel in the south, and I happened to be the star of her business." She paused to read his expression, but he was bland. She wasn't sure if he was listening or thinking of ways to abandon her once she was done. Either way, she had started this and would end it, no matter what.

"I started fucking men at the age of thirteen because I had no choice. I worked there for years until I mustered the courage to leave," she added.

His eyes were still on her, but this time, they were moist.

"Alex, that day you met me was the day I ran away from that life—"

Alex butted in, "That's enough, please."

Minnie kept quiet, allowing him to adjust to what she had just told him. But minutes passed, and when she could not stand the suspense, she spoke up.

"I'm sorry I never told you this."

He held his hand up. "Don't."

Her throat dried up as he staggered back from her.

"No more. I've heard enough," he said again.

She felt a hard, quick pulse in her throat and the tears in her eyes dried off immediately. All she could see or focus on was him, knowing she could not lose him. She moved to him, attempting to grasp his hands, but Alexander blocked her and turned away.

He walked on until he was out of the room while she stood dumbfounded.

Alexander left her! That was all that echoed in her mind.

Tears rolled down her cheeks as she realized her worst fears were confirmed. But she could not lose him.

So, she dashed out of the room with her clouded eyes as her heart throbbed with each passing second.

Minnie kept running until she saw him beside his car. His face was buried in his palms, and her heart lightened up. She ran to him and wrapped her arms around him.

"I am so sorry."

Against her expectation that he would push her off, he raised his head slowly as though he was surprised that she had come to him, but she did not want him to leave her.

Without thinking, she pulled herself to her toes, placed her lips on his, and kissed him with all passion and desires of her heart. At first, he stiffened, but he relaxed and pulled her closer to himself, heightening their kiss. He kissed her as though he never wanted to let her go. This was alright, as she didn't want to leave.

"Dominique?"

Tearing through the midst, Minnie shook as she heard Alex's voice behind her. At first, she was shocked that his voice was stern and furious, but on getting her senses back, she jumped away from the man she had been kissing when it hit her hard. Her eyes met with Andrew's, and shivers ran down her spine, and she spun around to Alex.

He had an icy stare on. He was angry, but most, he was hurt.

Totally shattered, Minnie blacked out.

Eight

How funny is life? Life, an endless cart filled with choices, possibilities, and moments. Of all possibilities she could have imagined, being granted the luxury of love was totally off her limits. How could she, a lowly slumcutter, imagine she could escape the realities of her life and be happy? After all, her fate had been sealed right from her birth. Why wish for happiness when she was nothing but the anchor of jumbles?

She had tried to tug a war against destiny, but as it should be, she lost. She wanted to be different and scrub off the permanent ink of her past, hoping a plain sheet could house all the emotions she desired to make. Yet, there she was, trapped in the darkness of her soul, soaring away into nothing. Maybe this dark space was perfect. There, she was away from their daunting words and spiteful glances. There, she could not hurt anyone or get hurt herself. She was destined not to be loved —that she had accepted.

At least the universe allowed her a glimpse of love, no matter how short-lived it was.

"Dominique?"

She heard voices call her from a distance, but this was so faint, as if she was far, far away from them.

"Minnie!"

The voices came in much clearer, and she could make out Alexander's voice. Following his voice, she pulled out of the dark void, listening to nothing but his guidance. Slowly she peeled her eyes open, but a dazzling light made her close them again.

Trying again, Minnie parted her eyelids and found that she was in a room. Standing beside her was Alexander's mother, and not too far was Andrew. She turned to the other side, her eyes met with his, and the incident gushed at her. From his cold appearance, she knew that he despised her. This was okay, as she despised herself too.

She parted her lips to speak, but all that came out was a wheeze of air. Someone placed a warm palm on her head, and she looked up to meet Abigail's face. Her face drew into a warm smile as she stroked Minnie's hair.

"You are still shaken. Do rest, okay?" Abigail said.

Minnie's lips stretched into a smile. "What happened?" she asked.

Abigail was about to reply when another female's voice spoke. "You fainted."

Minnie followed the voice and saw Madison standing in a corner.

"Maddie is right," Abigail said. "But you will be fine."

"Thanks." Minnie rasped.

"We are glad you're up," Madison spoke again

Minnie turned to her.

Madison had a tightlipped smile, and her eyes were moist. "Some of us were really scared," she added and glanced at Alex, who had his face fixated on the window.

He said nothing but huffed and stood from his seat.

"Where are you off to?"

Without replying to his mother, Alex walked out.

Minnie felt her heart drop, but she could not give up yet, could she? The fact that he was there when she woke meant he still cared for her. She would not stop till she got him back. To prove to him and everyone else that her feelings were true, she would fight to ensure nothing came between them again. Not his replica, his family, and not even the demons in her head.

* * *

Minnie awoke to the beautiful chatters of birds. It was then she realized she had slept. The room was quiet, indicating she was alone.

She got up and sat at the edge of the bed.

"You are up?"

She almost jumped out of her skin when she heard Matthew's voice behind her, and she stood and faced him.

"H-Hello…" She tried to greet him, but he scoffed.

"I don't need your greetings, girl."

Minnie swallowed her spit as she stared at him, her breath caught up in her throat.

"You should not be here. Hope you know that?" he asked.

She gulped hard but firmed up, determined not to break under the circumstance. Minnie straightened up and said, "I know you don't like me, but—"

He did not let her speak and said, "You are an opportunist looking for someone to cling to. You are like a parasite looking for a host to milk dry. You are hoping to get yourself a better life with this arrangement, right?"

Minnie could not believe her ears. She stared at the man, feeling his eyes burn right through her, displeasure reeking through them.

Not giving up, she stuttered, "I am not an opportunist!"

Matthew laughed. "Is that so?" he asked.

Rising from his seat, he strode to her, only stopping a few inches from her. "What do you call yourself then, Dominique, or should I say, Minnie, the sex worker?" he asked. "The girl that has been ravished by several men, including my brother."

Minnie felt a pang on hearing this, and she looked down, wondering how he found out about her acts with Vincent. But, no matter how hard she tried to push his words away, he was hell-bent and wasn't relenting.

"You are a slut, and you expect me, or anyone at all, to believe that you are saintly with a pure heart, looking for a second chance to be good. How can you deny not being an opportunist?" he asked and gave her a once over before scoffing. "However, you are hardly to blame, as Alexander was the foolish one to have taken a liking to you. My son, a dignified gentleman, cannot be with a nobody like you: a graceless orphan from the gutters, a sickening piece of shit, and a ravaged prostitute."

Her throat burned as she tried to subdue the tears that rose from within her. She felt like ripping her chest out to free it from all the hard truths of herself. Yes, Matthew

Canaan had said nothing wrong. He was right. She was everything he said and more.

"You are a gold digger, here to use my son for his wealth," Matthew added, his voice echoing deeper into her head.

Minnie could not agree with this. She could be anything. But, using Alexander for his money and hurting him, no. She would not hurt the only man who has ever looked past her physical body to find the timid young girl, confused and seeking nothing more than freedom. She loved him, which was the most real feeling she had ever had for anyone.

Slowly, Minnie lifted her eyes from the floor and faced the man squarely.

"With all due respect, sir, I must say you are wrong. Yes, I'm messed up. Yes, I'm a nobody, a filth, and a slut," she said as she moved to him. "But the one thing I am not is a gold digger."

With all the confidence she could muster up, she added, "I love Alexander with all my heart. If it's a crime for someone like me to love someone like your son, then fine, I'll do what you want. I will stay away from him to show you that I am not here for his money or your family's fame. I am only here because I love him, nothing else attached."

Matthew immediately said in a plain, austere voice, "Then leave."

Her words ceased in her throat as she blanched.

"If you are not an opportunist as you've stated, then leave right now," Matthew repeated. "Alexander despises you. You've got no more to do in the home and this family. So, with the last dignity you have, get out!" he said, and without another word, he walked out of the room.

Minnie was dumbfounded, but she did not do anything. Instead, she sat on the bed as moments she shared with Alex replayed themselves in her mind, and the outcomes of the past few hours, but her naïve-self kept wishing she was in a dream, and she would wake and find that everything was perfect.

This must be a dream. Or, how could she be so unfortunate, unlucky, and imperfect? Probably, God just made her a wreck simply for His amusement. She was just an example of a failed specimen of the Creator, a really messed-up creation.

* * *

Fingers snapped in her face, and Minnie jumped out of her thoughts. Standing over her was Andrew with a bemused look.

"You could wear off faster with all that thinking."

She rolled her eyes, purposely ignoring him. After all, this was partially his fault.

Minnie looked around and saw that she was outside the house, in the backyard. She sighed. She had walked out of the room but was so deep in her thoughts she hadn't realized that.

"Are you okay?" Andrew asked.

At once, bile rushed from inside her as she turned to him. He was the cause of most of her issues. He knew she could not run to kiss him, yet, he allowed her. He should have pushed her away. He could have slapped her, but he did not. If only he had been reasonable and sensible, then maybe, everything would have been different.

"What?" she yelled. "Why don't you just leave me alone? Why are you always in my throat, choking me?"

Andrew was undoubtedly taken aback by her outburst, but he was quick to rebound. "Listen, I just want to help—" He tried to speak

Minnie was done listening to him. "I do not need your help, Andrew," she spelled. "You have been the exact opposite of help to me."

"Dominique, I get that you are angered, but this isn't my fault," he said.

Minnie laughed. "Oh." She faced him. "But this is your entire fault, Andrew."

His brows pulled together as his face puckered. "How—?"

"How?" She chuckled. "Are you seriously asking me how?"

"Yes," he answered, "because none of this is my fault."

Minnie gasped. After everything, he still believed he was innocent. He was trying to play the saint when he was nothing close to being pure.

"You are an a-hole," Minnie snapped at him.

Surprised, he opened his mouth to cut in, but she didn't give him such grace.

"You knew I was not aware that you were the one standing beside Alexander's car. You knew I meant to kiss my boyfriend, but you—"

"I did not push you away," Andrew chimed in, completing her sentence. "Is that not what you wanted to say?"

His words echoed as the scene came pouring into her mind.

"How could I push you away, Dominique," he said. "Tell me, how could I when you have been all I've desired?"

Minnie froze.

"How could I resist you? How could I push you away when I want to have you tight to my chest?"

She was blank as she watched the words pour out of his lips. His hands gripped the side of her arms gently, causing her to look into his eyes.

"I shouldn't lust after my brother's girl, but I could not stop myself. I am well aware that you are Alex's, but I wish my reckless heart would hear of this. I might sound selfish, but I would not lie to myself, and neither would I do that to you."

His hands released her arms. He raised his palm to her face, placed his finger on her chin, and brought her face to his.

"I am sorry, Dominique, if this caused a rift between you and my brother, but I do not regret letting you kiss me."

Finally getting hold of herself, Minnie blinked repeatedly. She yanked herself from him, and her hand cut across his face with a slap.

"Pervert!" she spat and turned to leave before she could do more than slap his face.

Yet, he reached for her and pulled her back, saying, "I like you, Dominique."

Minnie laughed to herself. Andrew was crazy. She despised him, and she thought he shared her feelings. But this was impossible. Once again, she raised her hands to slap him across the cheek. However, this time, he held her hand in mid-air.

"I know you want to hit me all day, and I will not stop you, but I have to get these off my chest."

Minnie forcefully retracted her hand from his grip.

"Do you also know you are so stupid, Andrew?"

Surprisingly, he nodded.

"I do," he answered. "I am aware that I am the world's stupidest, but at least I am not a liar. I am not a bloody actor. I do not hide my feelings. I do not hide who I am, who I truly am."

She chuckled. "Yeah, who you truly are, indeed."

Then, she looked up until she was facing him squarely.

"Andrew Canaan, newsflash, who you truly are stinks!" she spat. "I love Alexander, and I will never stop loving him, no matter what!"

"Now." She poked him with her index finger. "These are my true feelings. The truest me."

With this, she turned and left. Not rethinking a thing, she moved to get her box and was soon out of the house.

Minnie kept her eyes on the gate and kept moving as fast as her feet could carry her away from the Ardor house, its madness, insane occupants, and the wild emotions boiling in her. She had no idea where she was going, but all she wanted to do was to keep walking. Yet, she could not break the force that kept drawing her back to the house. *I have to go.*

Maybe, all would be alright if she parted with them.

Never had Minnie thought to be the reason for anyone's hurt, but all her life, she had been hurting people. So many people she did not know had been hurt because of her. Yes, some were unintentional, but the fact remained that she had hurt them.

From the brothel, she had hurt other girls who had desired to be the stars of the sex world. She had outstarred them, inadvertently. Those men she had intercourse with who never stopped coming to the brothel, their wives and children were hurt as their father and husband left them every night to spend their savings on her. Oh, she must have broken several homes and relationships.

Now, she had hurt Alexander, and indirectly, she had also ended up hurting Andrew. In all totality, she had messed this family up too. It was definite she was cursed. This was the only explanation.

However, this was the punishment for all that. This was the price Minnie had to pay for being a sex tourist, a home breaker, a heartbreaker, a female, and for being herself.

Matthew was right. Maybe she was an opportunist. Maybe all she was searching for was attention. Perhaps all she wanted was to be loved by someone who would be gullible to believe all her lies.

They were all right. *I was using Alexander.*

Vincent was the innocent one, and she was guilty. After all, she was the tramp that lured him into her chambers with her half-naked body that night. The same went for Andrew, Alex, and other males with whom she had come in contact. It was none of their faults. She was the only one to be blamed. She was the irresistible female temptation. She was a mistake of creation, the cursed daughter of Jezebel, and a shattered destiny. This was who she was, and she could not be someone she wasn't.

Minnie had tried to change, but here she was.

She looked around, realizing she had walked far from the house. The Ardor house was no longer in sight. She was on the lone road, surrounded by trees and silence.

Moving to the side of the road, she sat on an abandoned wood log. She stroked it with her fingers as tears streaked down her cheeks.

She was like the log: broken, abandoned, useless, and redundant. She had been through life aimlessly. Never had she done a thing she would not regret later. She was terrible at controlling her actions.

Minnie had no one teach her what was right or wrong. She had no love and care from parental figures, making her open and indecisive. She was deprived of love; thus, it was easy for her to love Alex. Love was far from the fantasies she had dreamt of: love was pain, a lot of it.

However, this was how she had been, right? She did things without knowing the consequences, and then she was taught about it the hard way, but she survived. Life was her teacher, and she had to keep learning. All through everything, she knew she would be okay. She had to be fine. After all, "What doesn't kill makes one stronger." She would heal just like she always had.

Yet, she would run, as always.

Minnie stared at the road ahead, accepting the fate that awaited her. *This is probably for the best.*

She and Alex would have never really worked out. Minnie had hoped they would, but this was impossible. True happiness, love, and joy did not exist for someone like her. This was her reality, and it was high time she snapped out of her fantasies.

Minnie did not deserve a man like Alexander Jose Canaan.

With her muscles firmed, she wiped her face with the back of her hand and stood from the log. Taking a last glance back, she sighed.

This was the right thing to do, she knew.

"I am sorry, Alex. I'm sorry I came into your life and messed it up. I hope you will find it in your heart to forgive me," she said to herself.

"I hope you forget me, find someone better and more deserving of you. I love you so much, but this is the best for both of us."

However, her heart tightened, choking her as the throbs slowly overwhelmed her.

"Goodbye, Alexander," she added, as a tear streaked down her cheek, but she wiped it off and turned.

Taking a deep breath, she heaved and walked down the road.

Minnie had no idea where she was heading to. Neither did she have the foresight of what the future entailed. She couldn't tell what was waiting for her out there. She was oblivious to her destiny. But she trusted that she would survive, no matter what.

She must survive and keep going. There was no turning back. Minnie wanted to start anew, and this was what she must do.

Soon her steps turned into a jog and increased to a slighter run as she navigated her way down the lone road, heading towards wherever her feet led her.

Is this the end?

No, this is not the end.

The story has just reached its **climax** and the end of the first episode in the *Tales of Dominique.*

Next, we will follow Dominique as she wanders into life alone and is still haunted by the thorns of her past. In this struggle to overcome all she has been through and move on, she meets new characters who will either make her or break her.

It's not just about what Dominique needs. It's much bigger than what she has ever imagined.

This is just the beginning of all.

About the Author

Alexandra Oyelola was born in Northern Nigeria and lives in Kaduna State. She spends most of her time with her face buried in books, mainly kinesiology textbooks. She started writing when she could grip a pencil in her hand and has since explored the art of converting voices in her head into words that live through pages in the heart of her readers. Fascinated by romance with paranormal twists, Alexandra delights in reading and writing unconventional love tales to express her innermost self. She is an ardent procrastinator who aspires to complete a few things on her bucket list. Alexandra can be found at the pool when not writing or sleeping.

366 Days Together is her first novel published on Amazon.

Alexandra loves to connect with her readers:

Email: alexandraoyelola@gmail.com

Instagram: @alexandra_oyelola

Twitter: @temiloluwaalex1

Facebook: @alexandraruth.oyelola